HER DESTINY

Blake Jules

CONTENTS

CHAPTER 1

It's strange how your life can be written before you even take your first breathe.

How people can decide your fate even though they have never met you before.

That's what's happened to me, I'm Melody Wilhelm the daughter of the Mystical Wolf Maia Wilhelm and Alpha Austin Wilhelm.

People believed me and my three brothers to be powerful and to save the lives of all.

My brothers, yes. Me, no.

That's until I met my mate. The Alpha Prince.

This is my story. Of mates, tears and love.

____

"Melody. Push harder!" My Coach shouts as I push myself away from the cold wet grass beneath me.

He places a heavy leather boot on my back and presses down, making it even harder to complete my push up.

"PUSH!" He orders loudly before blowing a whistle. "You've done 298!"

I push against the force of his boot and bring myself away from the ground. The sweat drips form my nose onto the green grass under me.

"That's 299! Push Melody! Push!!"

My arms are shaking from my weight and my feet ache but I can't give up now. I only have 1 more to do.

I lower myself to the ground slowly trying to making sure not to go to low. The Coach's boot is heavy and try's to force me to collapse.

I fight back. Taking a final deep breath before pushing through my hands up against the boot.

I make it and finally allow myself to collapse into a ball of wheezes and sweat. I close my eyes and lie flat on my back trying to ignore the annoying voice of Coach.

"300 push ups, well done Melody. That's your new record, anyways next time you better get to 400 without any problems." He says right up close to my face "your next session is, of course, tomorrow. So see you then."

With a final evil smirk he wanders off leaving me in a my pile of sweat and exhaustion.

"Hey," I hear the familiar voice of my brother Mikey, who happens to be my older twin by 6.34 minutes. "You alright El?"

"Yes I'm great!" I say sarcastically, he laughs and extends his hand to me. I take it willingly and allow myself to be pulled to my feet.

"You're getting better." He says crossing his arms in front of his chest, showing his muscularity. Mikey had been training since he moment he could walk.

He is to be Alpha in 2 days. The ceremony is taking the pack into a total buzz of excitement and nerves. Gosh, you should see my mom.

"Mom given you grief about your mate today?" I say with a short laugh, he playfully punches my shoulder in reply.

"Of course she did! What a surprise!" He says putting an arm around my shoulder as we start walking, "She gives me the speech of how amazing it was for Dad to finally meet her and be at his very strongest.

Thank god I met Victoria a month ago or I would of had to get ear buds. Now I'm becoming Alpha too! Can I really do this?"

"Of course you can Mic!" I say slapping his chest, "you're ready for this."

"Thanks sis." He laughs and looks up with a sigh. I frown and turn to where his gaze is frozen. On the front steps of the academy, which is my home, is my father with a very strange look on his face.

"Melody. Mikey. You're finally home." My father says in a formal tone, he doesn't look annoyed close up but what could be wrong?

He gestures inside and quickly Mikey and I obey him. Once inside we are lead straight to our large private kitchen in our private part of the academy.

I see Joe and Tanner sitting at the table stuffing themselves with a bowl of Mom's famous pumpkin soup. They look up at Mikey and I with a smile before continuing to eat.

"Ah Mikey, Melody!" Mom says turning from the large pot on the stove. She toddles over to us and give us both a hug.

My mom is amazing, she has recently become a Pack Nurse. She always use to tell us how she was happy being a stay at home mom but as soon as Tanner turned 10 she wanted more.

Even though she is Luna, along with Luna duties she decided to take on a part time job at the infirmary.

My dad on the other hand is a full on Alpha. Constantly training wolves or in his office completing paper work. Sometimes he can be out (or in his office) for the whole day.

Although he is busy, he always makes time for us especially Mom. I swear sometimes they are like teenagers when they make out in the kitchen when I come down to eat breakfast.

"Sit down, a bowl of pumpkin soup each?" Mom says happily pushing me softly towards the dining table.

"Yes please mom." I reply taking a seat at our family table that holds 6 people. Perfect size right?

"Uh duh!!" Mikey says pulling a double chinned face while sitting at the end of the table next to Joe and myself.

As soon as Mom places the warm bowl of soup in front of me, all of my hard work today makes my stomach tumble in extreme hunger. I'd forgot to eat today.

I grab my spoon and shovel the hot amazingness into my mouth. It warms my throat and I sigh in content.

While eating I watch my father sit at the head of the table smiling gently. He turns to my mom and traced for her hand. She takes it and he drags her to her seat.

"Right, listen up guys." My father says. All five of us are instantly listening. "As you have probably heard the Alpha King's son is coming to visit our pack. It's nothing serious, he is just coming to see how our pack is doing and how we, as the Alpha Family, are running it."

I glance nervously at my siblings who I notice where similar expressions. We've always heard so much about the Royal Wolves but they never usually leave their pack, or don't tell people when they do.

"Okay, does this mean no pranks!?" Joe complains throwing his spoon into his bowl and leaning back in his chair.

"Joe! You don't need to prank anyone anymore!" I sigh, it really annoys me. Don't get me wrong I'm really close to Joe but he is constantly pranking and it usually always ends up with me in trouble.

"Yes I do!" He argues but I don't reply. We both shut up with one stern look from my father, I do not want to see him angry. He may be super amazing but if he gets annoyed, he really gets annoyed.

"As I was saying, the Alpha Prince shall be down for one night only. So it's my pleasure to announce that we will be holding a big grand ball in his honour. I've warned the pack and everyone is preparing." Father explains.

"Wait," I say shaking my head "what?!"

I turn to Mikey who is grinning, "time to ask some girls to the ball!" He winks at me making me let out a groan.

"Dumbass. Better not let Victoria here you!" I say under my breath but can't help but chuckle at his expression.

"When is this?" Tanner speaks up quietly, I only just realise he hasn't said a word this entire conversation.

"Well," Mom speaks up now, "in a days time. So Melody, dress up super love because there will be lots of new people there to meet and just maybe you'll meet your ma-"

"Mom!!" I squeak standing up abruptly "that's not fair! Oh great please don't tell me this is another set up for me to find my mate!! I'm not going to find him!"

I turn away from the table and ignoring all their shouts I rush away and upstairs to the roof. The roof is my escape. Nobody except my brothers know about this hiding place so I'm safe for a while.

Until my parents send out a search party...

You may think I'm over reacting but I came to terms with me not finding my mate when I was 16 years old.

I slowly take a seat on my small lonely wooden bench, darkness has found its way into the sky now and the stars have come out to play.

I look up at the twinkling lights in the blackened sky, stars are such an illusion. They look teeny tiny but in reality they are giant balls of burning gas.

I suppose parts of life can be an illusion as well. Like true love for an example, someone expects to find it so their mind creates the illusion for them. But it turns out he has been cheating for years and she is in love with another guy.

Life hurts.

With so much expected on me and training everyday I never got a proper teen life. I never got a high school boyfriend or even a date.

My life is a burning ball of gas deep in space and I can't seem to reach out and get it back.

"Knock knock." A familiar soothing voice says from the secret cubby hole. I turn with a smile to my best friend, James.

"Hey James." I say quietly which gives him the unspoken inviting to join me.

I fiddle with my fingers as he comes down and sits next to me. I look up with a soft smile and lay my feet across his lap.

"You okay?" He asks leaning his arm along the whole back of the bench.

"I don't know." I shrug "maybe I am. Maybe I'm not. You'll have to check back later." I say looking back up at the stars twinkling.

"I heard about the grand ball." He says punching my arm, "has the mother started?"

"Mother has started. Well she insinuated about meeting new people my mate by some miracle!" I laugh shoving him back.

"Well we are obviously going to have to get you a super smoking hot dress!!" He says giving me his evil smirk.

"You got a girl yet?" I ask looking straight at him, I know the answer to who he wants to take but has he asked her?

"Uh," he turns down to his lap "I think she is going with Brody."

"James!" I say slapping his chest "She is you mate for god sake!"

"I may or may not have not told her that we are mates...." he says standing up making me almost collapse onto my ass.

"No wonder you've been jumpy whenever you see her!" I scold myself for not noticing sooner. "Well you better tell her or I will because this is a once in a life time chance James! I don't even think I will have one but you have one so take her and never ever let her go!"

"Urgh when did you become Dumbledore?!" He groans slumping back down on the bench that creaks from the sudden weight.

"About 3 minutes ago!" I laugh standing in front of him "now give me a hug!"

He chuckles and squeezes me in a bear hug that I call the James-too-tight-hug. James is super tall and super muscular so compared to him I'm like a bloody mushroom.

"Well you better get back, I swear your going to give your parents a heart attack if you keep disappearing." James says pushing me towards the cubby hole.

"I don't want to!" I complain but oblige even if I am against going home and getting yet another talk from my parents.

The 'you the daughter of the mystic wolf so your life is in danger because you could be the next one' talk. Which I get everyday. I am not the mystic wolf, I am normal and I like it that way.

It's not like my mom talks about being the Mystic wolf at all or shows me. I just get the 'it's dangerous' and 'you could be next in line'.

Well no thank you.

I finally get to the Alpha wing and find my parents sitting on the couch awaiting. Oh great.

CHAPTER 2

I step further into the living room and my parents stand up looking directly at me. My father looks me up and down before sighing in relief.

"Thank god you're not hurt!" He says throwing his arms in the air. "You realise you could of been hurt."

"You've trained me since I was 5 years old, I think I can handle myself." I say shrugging then removing my shoes and placing them by the front door.

"Melody-" my mom says walking up to but I hold out my hand to stop her.

"I love you both, a lot. But I don't want this talk with you every time I walk through the door 5 minutes past curfew. I'm not 10 anymore, I'm 18 years old!" I say throwing my arms in frustration.

I feel the heat rising up my throats and I fear for what I would say. My parents don't deserve my anger. As they try to continue I throw my shoes back on.

"Melody please, stay here." Mom says trying to reach out for me. Father comes at me too but I stand up straight holding my arms up in the air.

"I can't, I promised James I'd help him out with Jessie. I'll be back by midnight, but please don't wait up and don't worry." I say giving them a small smile before opening the front door and walking out.

I walk down the corridor and pull my jacket tighter to my body. I greet people as I pass and try not to think of the fact that they will tell my parents where I am.

Everyone in the pack is so loyal to my parents, they love them. I'm glad I don't have the weight of the pack on my shoulders because it's just too much.

I finally make it to Oli's apartment and knock on the door frantically. I glance at my phone screen and see it's just gone 10pm.

It's late but I have to talk to somebody. James is busy and I don't want to bother Mikey right now. I know he has a mate of his own to take care of.

I jump as Oli throws his door open, he looks at me through half closed eyes. He is wearing a pair of pj trousers and his hair is disheveled. I woke him up, great.

Nice going dumbo.

"Babe?" He croaks as he opens his door wider allowing me to pass him into his apartment. His eyes follow me as I walk into his small cozy apartment.

"Hey Oli, sorry to bother you but I had to get out." I say rubbing my face with my hands.

"Hey hey, it's okay Melody!" Oli says closing the door and bringing me into his embrace, his arms are strong and I have gotten so use to being in them, so why does it feel confining? "What's up babe?"

"Just stuff, I'm fine just...um wanted to see you." I say trying to smile up at him, he gives me a smirk and plants a kiss on my forehead.

"You can stay as long as you want babe." He says rubbing my back soothingly but tonight it feels weird, like it burns my back.

I shake my head and ignore it, maybe it's because I'm angry. I need a run, my wolf hasn't been out for a while. Training has taken up a lot of my time recently.

'Not our mate.' My wolf says angrily, she has always been silent when I'm with Oli because she is angry that I'm not waiting for my mate. 'Need run.'

"Um no," I say getting out of his arms and heading to the door "um I have somewhere else I need to go, sorry for bothering you."

"Melody wait," he says grabbing my hand "don't go! You can spend the night, we can finally take the next step. I know you've wanted to wait but I really want you."

I flinch away from his hand and finally find myself getting scared. I've never thought of sex before, I was told to wait for my mate. But I don't want my mate? Or do I?

Why does it feel like today is going by super fast? I can't keep up with the drama and anger.

Why am I so confused tonight?!

"Look I'm sorry for bothering you." I apologise and feel bad for waking him up then running out, I mean he is my boyfriend "It's a big day tomorrow and I have to get ready."

"Fine." He says walking me to the door and slamming it after me, I let out a long sigh. Oli has always been the dramatic type.

It's only 10:30pm and I don't want to go home until I absolutely have to. Tomorrow is going to be big, my moms is going to make James take me shopping for a dress then my father is going to give me the 'I can't believe she is so grown up' speech.

I let out a laugh as I walk down the corridors, I may get annoyed at my parents but they are the best out there. My parents are my inspiration.

'Lody come home please? It's a big day tommorrow plus I have news!'

Mikey's voice pops into my head. I stop in my tracks in the middle of the dark corridor.

He sounds like he needs me, but do I want to go home yet. I still have time before midnight. The curious wolf in me comes out and I instantly want to know his news.

I let out a ear piercing scream when a hand grips my shoulder, a hand covers my mouth soon after. I turn my head and see that it's only James.

I smack his hands away from my face and push him slightly.

"James!" I growl in a low voice "what the hell are you playing at?!"

James, who is too busy laughing his butt off, grips my shoulder once again trying to keep himself from falling.

"Gosh, you should of seen your face!" He laughs holding his stomach "I haven't seen you this scared since you peed your pants in front of the whole school in kindergarten."

"Oh shut up James!" I whisper shout, I'm half annoyed but I'm finding his laughing funny too.

Mixed moods here.

"Mikey told me to find you." He says once finally farming down "plus I want to tell you to be up early! We're going-"

"Don't say it..." I mutter to myself closing my eyes to await the dreaded word.

"SHOPPING!" He laughs in my face, shaking my shoulders at the same time.

"You hate shopping James, and I hate shopping so why?!" I say banging my head against his shoulder in annoyance.

"Because," he says grabbing my shoulder and moving me to arms length so he can look me in the eye "you need a dress and I'm your best friend!"

"Fine, but if I'm being forced to get a dress you have to get a tux!" I say poking him with my finger, he gasps dramatically "with a bow tie!!"

"You are such a horrible woman!" He says punching me playfully "deal."

We do our famous spit shake which consists of; spit, shake, high five, high ten and a fist bump.

"Now I think I have a brother in need back at home!" I say pointing to the direction of my home. James gives me a big smile in return "hey you should invite Jesse along. People can change their mind about ball dates you know."

I give him one last hug and a tiny yap on his blushing face before heading back up to my home. The corridors are deserted and dark, I only meet a few male wolves who are on duty.

I finally get to the final corridor but come to a stop when I see our front door open. Mikey stands there with a smile on his face and Victoria is hugging him before waving goodbye and disappearing down another corridor.

"Mikey!" I shout as he turns to go back into the apartment. His head whips around and he sighs in relief.

"Melody where have you been?!" He says worriedly, as soon as I'm near his he quickly rushes me inside.

"I was at Oli's, what's going on?" I whisper standing in front of him. I give a quick sweep around the room and sigh as there is no sign of my parents.

"Well firstly, I'm glad your okay!" He says quietly standing close so we can hear each other "secondly, Victoria and I have decided to complete the mating process tomorrow night! We've marked but now all that's left is the actual mating." He adds a wink at his last remark making me want to roll my eyes.

He sounds so excited and I can see how happy he is, so instead of being a downer or complaining I pull him in for a hug.

"Congrats big bro!" I say happily "you deserve her!"

"Thanks Melody!" He says hugging me tightly, suddenly he pulls away and looks upstairs "Oh crab balls! Mom is up! Right don't tell mom or dad about Victoria and I yet!"

"Okay I won't promise!" I say rushing to say everything "now quick get upstairs!"

We both hurriedly make our way up the stairs trying to be quiet as we run. I watch as Mikey darts into his room safely and I'm about to open my door when my name is called.

"Melody." My mom calls from a few feet behind me, I freeze and slowly spin around.

"Mom." I greet pretending that I wasn't just running for my life.

"You okay sweetie?" She says pulling me in for what is my like 5th hugs in the last 2 hours.

"Yes I'm good, just exhausted after training and going out." I say hugging her back, she smells like roses and fresh bread.

"Well okay, get some rest now. I'm sure James had plans for you tomorrow." She says pulling away with her motherly smile, then kisses my cheek before wandering off back to bed.

I lean against the door and stare into the darkness of the corridor. In under 24 hours I shall be dressed up and dancing around the grand ball room.

What if I do find my mate? I've tried so hard to put the pressure of finding a mate behind me. I mean my mom is the Mystical wolf, and everyone expected me to be but I'm not.

I am a normal average wolf.

Suddenly a voice popped up in my head. 'We want our mate!' My wolf says stubbornly.

I do. I do want to find my mate, I'm scared of the outcome like most. But instead of wondering if their dead or already mated, I'm scared that I will let them down or reject them out of fear.

My phone starts ringing in my back pocket so I quickly bring it out and answer it straight away. It's Oli.

"Hello." I answer sliding down onto my floor against my bed. My body itches for a shower to clean everything away.

"Hey, I'm sorry for tonight." He says though the phone.

"It's fine." I say standing up and sitting on the edge of my bed instead.

"I wanted to ask you if you want to go to the Ball tomorrow with me?" He says and I hear a voice say something in the background making Oli sigh.

"Maybe, I don't know I'm sorry Oli. My parents probably want me with them representing the pack. I'll text you." I say rubbing my temples trying to decide.

"Okay, goodnight Melody." I hear the slight annoyance in his voice but I don't say anything about it.

"Goodnight Oli." I say before hanging up, I don't know what's wrong with me lately. I know we haven't been in the best place lately but I didn't realise we would be distant towards each other.

You need a shower Melody...

I think standing up and heading into the bathroom.

———————————

CHAPTER 3

I place my phone back onto my bedside table without replying to the messages. I stretch out my tiresome limbs and swing my legs out of bed.

I pad my way straight to the bathroom for a much needed shower. I let the water run cold over myself.

The freezing water bites at my skin awaking every nerve and bone in my body. I lean into the water and turn the switch to hot.

The warm water bursts from the shower head allowing each goose-bumps on my arm to retreat. I put my head under the water and close my eyes.

I quickly wash my hair then turn off the shower just in time to hear my moms voice at my bedroom door. I left my bathroom door open so it was fairly easy to hear.

"Honey! It's almost 7am, James is here!" She shouts in urgency, I sigh and grab a towel from the radiator. Safely wrapping it around myself I answer my mom.

"It's okay mom! He can come in!" I shout back grabbing another towel for my wet hair.

I hear the bathroom door open then close and James' scent hits me seconds after. I make my way out of the bathroom and find a grinning James laying on the bed.

My bedroom is a medium size with a bed, desk and a sofa that turns into a bed. Then I have three doors; one for my bathroom, one for my walk-in wardrobe and one for my bedroom door.

"Hey Lodi," he says sitting up from his previous position "shopping time!!"

I let out a long annoyed groan as I make my way into my walk-in closet to get dressed.

***

"James!" I laugh feeling my chest tightening from the amount of laughter.

I watch as he dances with someone dressed as Minnie Mouse in the middle of the mall. He finally finished and gives Minnie a big high five then runs over to me.

"That was so much fun!" He laughs patting my back preventing me from choking on my own saliva.

"You are such an idiot James!" I say slapping his over the head "Oh gosh, I think you have literally killed me."

He just laughs, picks up the bags then starts heading back to the car. I follow him still holding my ice cream cone, we ended up spending most of our time in the ice cream shop.

I got salted caramel and James got mint chocolate chip. I must admit the mall's salted caramel ice cream is to-die-for.

"Well that was a good shop, even if it took you like 4 hours to pick out a bloody dress!" James says throwing our bags into the boot of his car.

"Hey!" I say punching him playfully "I need the dress to be perfect, I'm not like all those other girls."

"Yes but did you have to take forever to pick one! You didn't even try on half of them. Just picked them up, looked for 20 minutes and put them back." He groans opening my door.

"Well I am sorry your majesty." I joke, poking my tongue out at him. I quickly get in before he shuts the door and gets in the drivers side.

"Well at least that's over." He says starting the engine, "oh I talked to Jesse."

I whip my head around to look at his sheepish blushing face and smirk. "And...?"

"Well she knows we are mates now, and she said she'd go to the ball with me!!" He says jumping up and down as much as he could without hitting his head.

"That's awesome James!! How come you aren't together mating?!" I say shaking his arm as he just starts turning beetroot red.

"She told me she wants to take today to tell people and decide what she wants to do about us." He says driving down the long road leading to the academy.

"Fair enough then." I say.

We drive in a comfortable silence with the soft beat of the radio in the background for the rest of our journey.

When we finally arrive at the academy, I see the wolves training hard and mothers taking care of their children in the play park.

My father stands talking to some of the top guards near the entrance doors.I unbuckle myself and get out of the car, I grab my bags from the trunk at the same time as James.

I look back at him after noticing he had stopped, he was smiling down at his phone. I grin and let out a cough to get his attention.

He looks up at me with a mischievous and extremely happy smirk on his face.

"I have to go, Jesse wants me to meet up with her." He says giving me and hug, then after untangling ourselves from each other's bags he rushes off.

I turn around and head into the Academy, my father gives me a small wave while I walk in which I return.

I head straight for my bedroom as soon as I get through the large double doors. I make it safely to my room without bumping into anyone.

I drop the load of bags on the floor at the end of my bed then effortlessly fall onto my bed. The comfort makes me sigh in relief, I've been on my feet all day so it's nice to get off them.

I sit up and rest on my elbows, I look at my digital clock by my bed. It's 12:35pm already, the ball doesn't start until 6 so all in all I have 5 1/2 hours to get ready.

I need food.

I think as my stomach let's out a long wail of hunger. I giggle then get up and head straight to my favourite destination, the kitchen.

As soon as I enter the kitchen, the scent of my moms famous home made cinnamon buns intrude my nose.

I sit down on the island drooling over the fresh batch placed right in front of me. I place my hand on one just to be slapped on the hand.

"Melody," mom says appearing out of nowhere "they are for later when your father gets back."

"Please mom!" I beg feeling the need for the cinnamon buns grow as they sit in front of me, daring and delicious.

"Fine." She huffs putting one on a plate "just the one!"

"Thanks ma!" I say happily giving her a kiss on the cheek then race upstairs to my room once again.

Time to prepare for the ball...

***

My mirror must be a fake, there is no way the person standing in front of me is actually me. It looks like me but different and strange.

I feel like I'm trying to be someone I'm not, but this person is beautiful and gorgeous. She is someone guys would go for or even date!

Her brown hair is curled into magnificent waves down over her shoulders. A shining silver diadem is placed carefully on my head.

Her silver eyes stand out against the thick black mascara and eyeliner. Her lips and a natural pale pink, making them look plump and kissable.

My dress is stunning. It's a two piece, the top half is a pink and white blend and finished above her breasts, from there and over the shoulders it is see through with sequins placed methodically on it.

The bottom half is the same pick blend as the top half and it falls behind me slightly as I walk. The strap around my waist matched the sequins from the top half.

My should are silver high heels that make her tall and majestic.

That's me.

I think standing proudly in front of the tall large mirror. I give myself a nod before turning around and leaving the guest bedroom.

I meet James down the hallway, he is dressed up in a nest black tuxedo with his hair gelled back into a perfect placement.

"Well look who is looking gorgeous for once!" James says grabbing my hand and spinning me around.

"Uh says the guys who thinks any t-shirt and jeans counts as formal!" I say slapping his chest playfully before we start heading towards the ball hall on the other side of the academy.

It's usually used for dance classes but it's meant for formal balls or celebrations. My 18th birthday was held in the very same hall.

"Where is Jesse?" I say swinging my arms slightly as I watch James walking with his arms behind his back.

"I told her I'd meet up with her outside the ballroom door." He says giving me a beaming smile "I can't wait to see her!"

I let out a giggle and link arms with my best friend, we walk in complete sweet silence and the long corridors are quiet and lonesome.

We arrive at the ballroom doors in a matter of minutes, I see Jesse standing by the door waving frantically at James.

Her cherry red hair is pulled tightly up into a large bun, filled with purple flowers. Her emerald green eyes shone as she watched James approach.

Her dress is a deep violet purple that flows down to her ankles show-ing her black high heel shoes. I notice her eyes drift to my arm that is linked with James'.

I let go of James and give him a smile, he looks down at me with an even bigger smirk. "I'll see you later." I say and he nods before walking ahead of me slightly.

"Hey!" She says hugging James as soon as he reaches her, I give her a smile then walk straight past them into the ballroom.

It takes my breath away. The ballroom looks more elegant and amaz-ing than it ever has before. There is a table to the side filled with the most fantastic looking drinks.

The ballroom floor is polished and sparkling as people dance to the music. The orchestra is playing the the side of the room, they have created an small audience around themselves.

On the roof there is hanging white clothes that remind me of snow and icicles. There are white lights on the tall ceiling making it look like stars.

I smile and walk further into the crowded room, I spot my parents in an instant. They are together talking to a big group of whom I think are other Alpha and Lunas.

My eyes scan the room further and I find Mikey in the middle of the ballroom slow dancing with Victoria. He notices me and gives me a cheeky wink before spinning his mate around once more.

"Melody!" I hear my little brother Joe shout from behind me, I turn and watch him run up to me with Tanner close behind. They are both wearing normal clothes, making me suspicious.

"Hey boys!" I say giving them both a hug, Joe is smiling like and idiot and Tanner is blushing. I raise an eyebrow at him but he looks away.

"We snuck down to see what it's like!" Joe whispers in my eyes excitedly, I let out a chuckle and look around the room.

"Tracy was asleep," Tanner adds "we snuck past her!"

"Oh right," I say shaking my head "well guess who is coming to get you instead!" I let out a laugh as the boys sleeping turn around.

"Hey mom." They say in unison and they sound like two puppies who've had their favourite bone taken off them.

"Come on you two rascals, back up to Tracy!" Mom says picking up Joe and holding onto Tanner's hand "Melody, go tell your father I'm putting them back to bed then enjoy yourself!"

I watch with a smile as my mom leads my baby brothers off to bed, where Tracy will most likely get told of for sleeping.

Uh oh.

CHAPTER 4

I slowly make my way around the ballroom wall towards where my father stands laughing with some other men and their mates.

"Father!" I shout as I get close enough, he turns his head towards me and smiles graciously.

When I'm close enough he pulls me into the circle of men and introduces me "gentlemen this is my daughter Melody! Her twin brother Mikey shall be taking over as Alpha next week!"

I smile and shake hands with all the strong Alphas, the atmosphere in this circle is strong and quite intense. Good thing I'm of Alpha blood otherwise I think I would of panicked.

"Uh father," I say finally getting to talk to him alone for a minute "mom has just gone to take the boys back-"

"It's okay!" The familiar feminine voice makes me jump from behind me "I'm back, Tracy has got them!"

"Well thank you Melody!" Father laughs taking my Mom's arm "now wait here, the Royals are about to come in."

I can't help the nervous shiver that creeps up my spine at his words, I shake it off and reply with a nod.

Suddenly my father's head guard, Paul, stands at the top of the stairs to the grand entrance to the ballroom.

The stairs are like from Cinderella. Two doors either side with a set of steps in front of each on a high balcony. Then on a middle balcony the stairs meet. From there straight down is another larger flight of stairs.

"Ladies and Gentlemen, may I introduce your highnesses Alpha King Russell and Luna Queen Kate!" He says loudly before stepping out of the way.

The whole crowd bursts into a fit of loud applause as the trumpets play loudly and the grand doors both sides fly open revealing the wolf King and Queen.

I'm surprised by how extraordinary they actually look. On the left The King has his crown resting proudly on his head of grey hair. On the right the Queen has her tiara placed on her flowing dark black locks.

I watch utterly mesmerised as they walk down the two staircases and meet in the middle. They greet each other with a smile before linking arms and turns to face us.

Everyone bursts into rounds of applause as they bow then move to the left. Everybody turns to the right side top door, I look around confused.

Did I miss something?

Paul comes back out from hiding and shouts "Ladies and Gentlemen, may I now introduce your highnesses and future Alpha King, sir Jayden Beaumont."

The grand doors open revealing a man of god-like quality. His shoes are formal and his trousers match the black of his shoes.

He's wearing a white t-shirt which allows me to faintly see his amazing drool-worthy abs and chest.

His jaw and cheeks bones are sharp and well defined. His mouth is pink and moist, ready to kiss. His face is bare of any beard or moustache.

His hair is jet black like the darkness of night, it's short on the sides then long and waved on the top. It falls over his eyes and he flicks it away flawlessly.

Finally I look at his eyes, electric ocean blue that sends sparks running up my spine and my wolf howling in amazement.

'Mate!' She howls in utter joy.

My heart stops. My blood runs cold and I look away from his intense eyes. My head is spinning with the new information, I have a mate.

I actually have a mate. And he is standing across the room from me.

I'm not alone anymore. But wait, he is the future Alpha King.

Oh cream puffs...

I watch as he walks down the staircase towards the middle where his parents stand. I watch how he walks with pride and power, with his arms down by his side.

Suddenly he stops halfway down the red carpet stairs and sniff the air. My wolf is skimping in glee as everyone hears his next word that makes my heart drop.

"Mate!" He says starring right into the crowd, his eyes are scanning so I quickly duck behind someone so he doesn't see me.

His voice sends pleasuring shivers up my spine. My wolf is going absolutely mental in my head making it hard to concentrate on anything other than him.

Everyone is whispering and applauding, I take the opportunity and race towards the exit trying to avoid the eyes of my mate.

I successfully make it, well I thought I did until I hear his sexy voice once more shout "stop her!"

I turn to see him staring at me while rushing down the large red carpet steps. Everyone turns to stare at me and I see a few people heading towards me.

They must be members of the Royal Crescent Pack.

I hitch my dress up and run towards the exit as fast as I could in heels. I fling the doors of the academy open and rush out of the academy.

I hear his footsteps getting closer and closer every second. His scent alone if making my wolf try to turn me around and leap into his arms.

I shake my head and allow my shoes to fly off as I run. I arrive at the steep drop that we always called Devils Hill because of the scariness of the slope.

For once I thank the Moon Goddess for allowing me to have this advantage of this slope, it'll help me gain some speed. All of a sudden the heavens open up above and pour the cold rain down.

The Thunder rings through the trees and the lightning momentarily stops me in my tracks. In the single second I stopped wet arms wrap around my waist and tackle me to the ground.

The electricity spreading through my skin is amazing, almost making me moan in pleasure. Suddenly Devils Hill which was originally an advantage has now changed as together, my new mate and I tumble and roll down the muddy hill.

My dress was absorbing all the squelchy mud making my body heat decrease on every roll. After what seems like hours we find ourselves at the bottom. I come to a hard sudden stop and lay flat on my back with my eyes closed.

The rain was beating down, hitting my face and going into my open mouth. I breathe deeply as my whole body aches from the tumbling.

"Mate." His voice is above me now, inches away from my face. I can feel his warm breath fanning my neck and I hold back a moan. His hands find my waist and I squeal at the electric tingles spread through my whole body at his touch.

"Mate." He repeats nestling his head completely into my neck; I feel my wolf jumping up and down in my head in complete excitement and awe for our mate. No! I don't have a mate! I don't! I realized that years ago, when I had to sit and watch others at 16 finding their mates, settling down and showing it off to everyone.

"Open your eyes." His sexy voice sends pleasuring shivers down my spine. My eyes unwillingly flutter open to see his beautiful face inches from mine now.

My eyes are on his lips which makes him growl lustfully at me, my eyes slowly move up towards his own and I gulp down my nerves. I meet his eyes and gasp at their beauty; they are bright electric blue unlike my own silver grey ones. My mouth utters a word that I never thought would escape my mouth.

"Mate." I whisper my eyes capturing his like a photograph that will always be in my mind. He smirks down at me and I watch how the rain drips from his nose and lands on my cheek.

His hands grip tighter against my waist making me breaks out of my spell. I push him away, making my shelter form the rain disappears. The cold water pelts down against my bare skin as I hear him growl and I stand up.

"Why did you do that?!" He says angrily walking back towards me, he try's taking me back into his arms but I slap them away. He growls deeply at me, he's getting annoyed because I'm not acting his way I should when finding my mate.

I stand up straight trying to control my nervous heart and uncontrollable wolf. He watches me closely as we stand apart in the rain.

Thunder bursts from the sky making me flinch; I've always been scared of thunder and lightning.

Ever since I was little. My body was shivering now and my teeth are chattering loudly. My dress is covered in mud and soaked with rain. I'd lost my shoes whilst running but they weren't my top thought at the moment.

Jayden takes a step towards me and I see the confusion and hurt in his eyes as I step away. My gaze falls to the ground.

"Love, what's wrong?" He says stepping closer once more but this time I don't move, my whole body is frozen with this new feeling.

The feeling of having my mate so close. The feeling that I want to run into his arms and never leave them. The feeling of wanting to have his lips on mine.

"I-I can't do this right now." I say shaking my head while avoiding his gaze. It would be difficult to tell him this if I was looking into his eyes.

"Do what?" He asks and suddenly his hand is on my chin, he slowly lifts it to meet my eyes.

"Be your mate." I say trying to look away but his grip was strong and firm on my chin. I can't deny the electricity flowing through me at his simple touch.

"Why not, love?" He asks dipping his head into my neck, it distracts me from my own thoughts and for a moment I think of giving into my thoughts.

"Because I-" a moan rips out of my mouth cutting me of as Jayden places a kiss on my sweet spot on my neck where I should bare his mark. I feel the prick of his canines and my heart stops completely.

He is going to mark me, oh cream puffs! I place my hands on his chest and while trying to ignore the fact of how absolutely amazing they feel I push him away.

I put my hand over my neck and look at him with my eyes wide. His face hold bewilderment and anger, he once again steps closer to me and lets out a small growl.

"Why'd you push me away this time?" He says annoyed, I gape at him and try to get my brain working again.

"You were trying to mark me!!" I say trying and failing to not sound surprised.

"Well yes." He says smirking and stroking my cheek gently "That's what you're meant to do when you first meet your mate."

"Not when they've just told you they can't do this!" I scream as the rain starts pouring down heavier, my body is shaking with shivers now.

"You are my mate!" He says gripping my waist tightly "You are mine and nobody else's. My soul belongs to you as yours belongs to me. You are going to be by my side forever because if you aren't I will kill anyone to get you there." I gulp down my nerves at the complete seriousness in his voice.

"But-" I say but he cuts me off, I let out a huff of annoyance.

"-no buts. You are moving into the castle immediately, you are my mate and future Luna Queen so you have to be protected." He says holding my hand, he starts walking back up Devils hill and dragging me along.

We start slipping and sliding back down after every step up the steep slope. Suddenly I slip completely flat and groan in pain.

"Love, you okay?" Jayden says quickly picking me up and holding me bridal style. I lean into his warming touch as my eyes start to close. Need to get warm.

CHAPTER 5

I wake up feeling a hand on my forehead, I let out a grunt and slap it away as sleep still clouds over me.

"She's awake." I hear my mom's familiar soothing voice, I shake my head and feel like sleeping for longer but then another voice speaks up making butterflies erupt in my stomach.

"Finally." He says making my wolf yearn for his touch, for the warmth he brings my body and the relaxation. How far away is he? He sounded distant.

I open my eyes to the white ceiling of the academy, I notice the chandelier and instantly know I'm in the main common room.

I blink quickly trying to wake myself up, I slowly sit up and hold my head whilst I do. I shake my head and look around, allowing my eyes to readjust from my sleep.

Sitting on the edge of the sofa where I am sat is my Mom and my Father stands close by. On the sofa opposite is James, Mickey and Victoria.

Jesse sits on the single chair next to James holding his hand tightly. I smile at my best friend, they are just so cute.

A cough echoes around the room and everybody turns to the person standing in the entrance arch. I gulp at the sight of Jayden standing there, topless with dishevelled wet hair.

His scent is so strong making my wolf pure in delight, I glance at his dangerously low hanging joggers and growl mentally. Nobody but me should see him like this.

Stop it. I mentally scold myself. I don't have a mate.

I feel a chill on the my legs so I look down and realise I'm wearing a t-shirt I've never even seen before. May I point out I'm only in a t-shirt and underwear.

"It's his top." Mikey says with annoyance lacing his voice as he nods to Jayden who is staring at me with an emotionless expression.

"What happened?" I ask as I set half naked in front of my family and friends. I pull at the bottom of the t-shirt nervously while waiting for an answer.

"You ran out on the ball." My mom says grilling my hand "Jayden followed you. We don't know what happened but he brought you back here. You were soaking wet, cold and past out."

"Oh." I whisper rubbing my temples to try and rid myself of the headache forming in my head.

"Jesse and I put you under the hot shower," Victoria says giving me a smile "then we tried changing you but your mate wouldn't let you wear anything other than his clothes. The joggers didn't fit you so..."

"How are you feeling?" James asks looking at me with worry evident in his face.

"Physically or Mentally." I reply standing up and looking around the room. Jayden is still standing in the same place but now his eyes are fixed on James angrily.

I watch him and notice his fists clench and his jaw tightening as he watched James watching me.

I let out a long sigh that grabs his attention straight away, I swear he got whiplash from how hard his head turned.

I give him a short smile and he comes straight over to me. His arms fasten around my waist like a seatbelt as he sit down next to me before actually pulling me onto his lap.

I squeak in surprise before frowning at him, I try to pull myself away and out of his lap but he growls in my ear.

"Don't." He seethes as his grip tightens around my waist. I feel his hot breath in my ear and I have to suppress a shiver.

I look up at my parents who give me a reassuring smile. I shake my head slightly and look down at my lap.

"Melody." I hear my youngest brother Tanner walk into the room, I look up and smile at him "Why is he doing that to you?"

I follow where Tanner is pointing to where Jayden has his arms wrapped around me. I turn my face up to his and see that his eyes are on me.

"Because he is her mate Tanner, now finish your homework or I'm turning the wifi off!" My mom says with a short laugh as Tanner races up the stairs.

He is her mate.He is my mate.

Oh sweet ninja turtles, he is actually truly utterly my real mate. He is the Alpha Prince.

I can feel myself starting to hyperventilate as all these thoughts raced through my head, getting blurrier and blurrier every second.

I clutch my chest as it burns for oxygen, oxygen that I cannot get.

"Melody!" His sweet voice makes my body try to calm down but it just reminds me that he is my mate.

I'm going to have to move in with him. That means I'll be leaving my whole life behind. I'll be leaving my parents, my brothers and all my friends.

What if I never get to see them again? What if Jayden locks e up in the castle like the Beast did to Belle?

What about my heat? I hadn't even thought about that. In a few weeks time I will go into heat and will have to mate with Jayden to stay alive.

The Moon Goddesses created heat to make sure mates give themselves to each other like they should for them to be happy and live a wonderful life together.

"Love, breathe." His arms are rubbing my back now instead of around my waist. His face is right in front of mine and I can see the worry in his shimmering blue pools.

I focus on his eyes and try my best to breathe, in and out. I breathe again but this time deeper but never once looking away from his eyes.

Soon I regain my breathing and feel my heart rate return to normal. I look around and realise I'm in my bedroom with only Jayden for company. I'm sitting on my bed with Jayden close by.

I lean back into my bed and let out a long sigh, I glance at the clock to see it's only just gone midnight. It feels like I've been here for months already.

"Melody," Jayden speaks up softly, I look at him and his face is in a frown as he watches me "are you alright?"

He is still shirtless and my eyes keep begging to take in those amazing abs but I stick to his eyes once more.

"I don't know." I reply honestly, playing with my bedsheets.

I watch as he crawls up the bed to lay beside me, he places a hand on my hip and I hold my breath. He slowly turns me onto my side to face him.

"Do you accept me?" He asks suddenly, looking at my mouth for a second before returning to my eyes, my heart stops.

Do I accept him?

I suppose in reality I would die without him but I could reject him but that could kill both of us if not just one of us.

I can't kill him, the mate bond has already started entwining us together. I can feel it deep within me, I feel the power he holds and the power I will hold starting to grow in the pit of my stomach.

"Do you accept me?" I ask him as my reply, his hand reaches out and grabs my fidgeting one. He brings it to his lips and places a chaste kiss on my knuckle.

"Yes." He says then placed another kiss on my knuckle "You are my mate Melody and one day my Luna, I am yours just as much as you are mine."

I allow myself to give him a smile in return but I don't open my mouth to talk. If I do I will muck everything up.

A knock on the door saves me from having to answer, I hear a growl from Jayden before he shouts for them to come in. He takes a seat next to me on the bed and tries to put an arm around my waist but I quickly slap it away.

I watch the door open to reveal not just my parents but the King and Queen. I quickly start to get up to bow as I was taught but Jayden pulls me back.

I frown at him but all he does is stare straight ahead at our parents standing in front of us.

I look at my mom and all of a sudden I just want to run into her arms and hugs her and cry. This day has drained my mental and emotional state so much.

"Jayden." The King says smiling at his son then turning towards me "Melody."

"We've come to see...well to see what you two plan for the future." My father says clapping his hands awkwardly, my mom grabs his hand and gives him a reassuring smile, one she has perfected over the years.

Wait, plan for our future?

Excuse me, I only met my mate like 5 minutes ago and now suddenly I'm suppose to know our whole future. Well that's not happening.

"As you know son," the King says still giving us a happy smile "we will be leaving in the morning for the castle, you must decide what you two are going to do."

"She's coming to the castle."

My mouth hits the floor as the words fly out of his mouth so naturally. I gape up at him but his face doesn't hold any emotion except determination.

"Excuse me?!" I say standing up fast so he can't pull me down again. I look at my parents who look shocked but they are smiling.

Why are they smiling?! My mate has just told me I'm moving to the castle in the morning and they are smiling!

How did I get myself into this mess?

"You hear me Melody," Jayden's says getting annoyed, I really need to watch his temper "you are moving to the castle."

"Uh let me rephrase myself, no I'm not." I say folding my arms over my chest, Jayden's eyes follow my movement and he growls lustfully.

I realise I am accidentally pushing my breasts out but I just growl back at him. He is not forcing me into this.

He stands up abruptly and raced past our parents who all look uncomfortable and awkward at the point. He stands in front of me and I can feel my heart starting to race from his close proximity.

"Yes you are." He says grabbing my shoulders roughly "You are my mate Melody, whether you like it or not. I realise you don't want to rush into anything so I will wait for you as long as you want. But my condition is you move to the castle, and it is not a request."

I look up at him in shock as he words ring through me like a siren. My head pounds at this whole situation.

He will wait for me, I don't have to mate with him straight away. I can take my time.

I have to leave home, I have to leave all my friends and family behind. I hope he lets me visit often or let's them visit.

I'm going to be Luna and not just any Luna either, the Luna Queen.

But can I really do this?

It's so much work and pressure to put on myself. In the future, if I go through with this, I will have Royal duties and that will include providing an heir for Jayden. It makes me sound like a baby bank.

I'm not accepting that. I will not have a baby because the royals want an heir, I will have a baby when I think the time is right. That is one thing right now that I know for sure.

I look up into Jayden's darkening ocean pools and let out a long sigh. His eyes become softer and softer as he stares into my own.

"Fine." I say, knowing that this will now change everything.

CHAPTER 6

T oday is the day.

The day I've dreaded the whole sleepless night. I can't stop thinking about it, it's racing around my head like a motorcycle.

Jayden moves from the sofa across the room, his handsome sleeping figure looks so peaceful in sleep and it makes my heart beat faster.

After I regretfully accepted to take off to the castle with him this morning, my parents tried to argue for me to stay but Jayden was having none of it.

After a few more hours of arguing, slamming doors, tears and sighing they all left for bed. Except Jayden who refused to be in a separate room from Melody.

So he ended up of the sofa bed, after an argument over him sleeping in the bed.

I know we are leaving in a few hours and I have to say goodbye to everyone and pack too. But I can't, it would make this into reality.

Reality is complicated and sometimes completely and utterly wrong. But dreams are what I want, my dream was to study and become a pack doctor eventually.

I was about to start going to classes and having some experience with the Lead Pack Doctor in the Academy. And I couldn't wait.

But reality soon came knocking at my door with a pretty big package. That package was Jayden, and his power, wealth and even a freakin' castle!

I have always been a dreamer, but a realistic dreamer. After finally putting my mate behind me along with the reality that deep down I knew everyday that I must have one.

I shake my thoughts out of my head and focus on seeing everyone before I leave. I lean over and grab my phone from my bedside table.

I glance at my unread messages and curse loudly, Jayden voices out of bed growling around the room. His dark slightly sleepy eyes wander around the room until they land on me.

"You alright?" He asks walking over and sitting on the edge of my bed. I watch his every move and my thoughts become inappropriate as I stare at his bare chest.

"Um...yes I'm o-okay." I say taking a deep breath "but I forgot some really serious things, firstly yesterday my brother was meant to be crowned Alpha but the royals showed up and it had to be postponed, I haven't even asked how he feels about that. He is my brother!"

"I'm sorry." Jayden says putting a hand on my arm comfortingly "Why don't you go see him right now?"

I try not to focus on the tingles coursing up my arm as I decide to nod in reply because I don't trust my voice.

"Was there anything else?" He asks looking directly into my eyes now, his ocean pools glow with the morning sun.

Should I tell him the second reason?

The second reason is Oli, I look down at the 3 messages he sent me.

I put my face into my hands and let out a long frustrated sigh. I feel Jayden move closer as he takes me completely into his arms, I revel in them until reality crashes into me again.

He is making me move away from everyone I love. I push him off his me and he lets out a loud annoyed growl, but I just growl back.

"I need to go out." I say standing up at last, I rush straight to my walk-in wardrobe avoiding Jayden's reaching arms.

I shut the door on him successfully then let out a sigh. I quickly refocus in meeting up with Mikey and Oli, that's what I have to do in my first hour out of the few I have.

I grab some clean undergarments before throwing on some black jeans, a comfy grey sweater and some simple white converse.

After cursing and storming around my closet trying to find my brush and figuring out what to do with my hair, I decided to put it in a milkmaid bun.

I finally walk out of the closet Goan empty bedroom, a note laying on the bed caught my eye and I guess it is from Jayden.

I pick it up and smile at the messy hand writing in front of me, it's just like I would of imagined his hand writing to be like.

Gone to a meeting with your father and my own. Meet with your brother and do whatever you need to, I'll make sure we won't leave until 1 this afternoon.-J

I can't help the smile that's finds my face, at least he cares I suppose. I could of landed with a mate who is careless.

I put the note down onto my bedside table then leave the room to find my brother. Considering his bedroom is across the hall I found him pretty quickly.

After knocking on the door he answers with a smile.

"Good morning!" He says cheerfully leaning against the door with a big grin on his face, suddenly out of nowhere Victoria pop up from behind him.

"Hey Melody!" She greets snuggling into Mikey's side, I internally grimace as my own mate flashes into my head.

"Hey you two!" I smirk poking them both in the stomach "So is this your first official day as Alpha and Luna?"

The brightness in their face told me that they were happy, they glanced at each other before shaking their heads.

"No tomorrow." Mikey answers "we fully mated last night so Father gave us the day off to spend time with each other."

I gape at both of their glowing faces before screaming in excitement and pulling them both in for a big sandwiched bear hug.

"Oh my gosh, I can't believe it! Congratulations guys!" I reply pulling away and looking at them. Now I understand why they are so over the moon happy.

My phone buzzes in my pocket making me break out of our happy little conversation. I grab my phone and sigh, its from Oli again.

I lock my phone and push it into my back pocket along and try to put everything else that I don't want to deal with today in there as well.

"I have to dash!" I say hugging them once more before making my way down the corridor "Congratulations again!"

"Thanks!" They chorus just as I tune the corner, the corridors seem reasonably busy today. I get caught with incoming hugs and farewells by basically every pack member I meet on the journey to the lobby.

I make it there just in time because Oli looks like he is about to storm off.

"Oli!" I say as he starts moving towards the academy doors, he turns to me and greets me with a warm smile. Oli and I have been together for a while now and suddenly cold water splashes me in the face.

I'm breaking up with him to mate with my Alpha mate. Leaving him alone and I probably won't see him in a long time. Les just hope we can leave on a high instead of him making it dramatic.

"Hey." He says giving me a gentle hug, I squeeze him before pulling away. "Shall we sit?" He asks pointing to the nearby sofa.

I smile at the sofa he heads to, it's a black sofa that's been there for as long as I can remember. It's started to get ripped and broken but I won't let my parents get rid of it.

This sofa is actually where I had my first kiss. It was a very awkward experience I have to say, it was with my middle school boyfriend Darren.

We were sitting waiting for his parents to come and pick him up. When suddenly he leans forward and pecks me on the lips.

I don't know why or how but instead of smiling or kissing him again, I sneezed. I don't mean the small casual sneeze, I mean the snot-on-the-walls sneeze.

I think he ran out crying after that, I was scared of sneezing in front of people for over a year after that.

Back to reality Melody.

I mentally thank my brain for ridding the thoughts of that memory. I follow Oli to the sofa and take a seat next to him.

I turn slightly to face him and wait for him to speak politely. As I wait for him to prepare, I notice a familiar scent floating around the air.

I grimace as my wolf reminds me of who it is by leaping up and down. I look at him in my peripheral vision, he is talking to my father on the other side of the lobby.

Any second now he will smell me, if he hasn't already. I don't want him to see me with Oli because it'll bring up questions that I don't want to answer right now.

I quickly turn back to Oli and try to keep Jayden out of my view. My wolf is already trying to make me run over to him and kiss his amazing lips.

Damn it!

"So," Oli says and I give him a encouraging smile "you found your mate."

"To put it lightly, yes." I nod biting my lip in anxiety, I suffered from anxiety a lot as a kid actually. But never mind about that.

"He's Jayden Beaumont, yes?"

"Uh yeah he is." I nod again feeling my heart race as his presence is becoming more well known to my wolf. I can sense him moving out of view and it's making my spine freeze.

"This is a lot to take in Melody." Oli says running his hands down his face. I grip his wrists and bring them to my lap, I take his hands into mine and give him a grin.

"I know Oli, trust me I know. But I suppose we both knew deep down own of us would find out mates one day. That's why we never mated or even talked about going there." I say rubbing his hands with my thumbs.

"Yeah I know but, being honest, I thought it was me who would find their mate first not you. You were always talking about never finding your mate and living your life happily without one." Oli says, obviously frustrated.

"Yeah, I know Oli. I'm sorry, I truly believed to be mate less. Look I'm moving to the castle today, I know it's difficult to understand this right now. But Oli your an amazing guy, you'll find someone else. Heck! You may happen to find your mate tomorrow. The world is full of surprises even if your not quite ready for them."

Oli gives me a hundred dollar grin and brings his hands and mine up to kiss my knuckles.

"Thank you. Melody Wilhelm, I will never forget this time we spent together." He says and I give him a peck on the cheek.

"I will never forget the time you tried to make me a bubble bath and fell in!" I laugh and his face falls "I swear the bathroom was flooded for like 2 weeks after that!"

"Hey!" He says punching me playfully "your father wanted my head for that! I was only trying to be nice!"

I laugh even more at the puppy eyes he tried to make, he soon joins in and I feel sad. I'm going to miss Oli.

Even if Oli was always dramatic and lately has been trying to take the next step, he has always been there for me.

He is the greatest best friend I could ever have.

"Friends?" I ask leaning in and capturing him in a tight hug.

"Best friends, Melody." He replays chuckling in my ear, I let out a giggle before a cough makes me pull away.

I look up into angry darkening ocean pools and freeze.

"What's going on here then?"

CHAPTER 7

His eyes are full of anger but the scary part of they aren't looking at me. They are glaring at a very frightened looking Oli.

Oli's hands squeezes mine and I try not to wince at the pain he is causing them. I let go of his hands immediately as Jayden's hardened eyes linger at them before returning to Oli.

I stand up abruptly and his eyes snap to mine. I stare into his eyes trying to not show any fear, he growls lowly and wraps his arms tightly around my waist.

I let out a long sigh but don't make a move to get out of his old in fear of him attacking Oli who has decided to stand up and glare at Jayden.

Even though Jayden is a good head taller than Oli and much more bulkier. Oli didn't seem to care, but that all changed when Jayden snarled.

His snarl made the walls around us shake and I physically had to grip his t-shirt tightly to stop myself from falling.

The ferocity and Alpha in his snarl made everyone in the room stop what their doing and bow while showing their necks in submission. Even me.

He glances down at me and his hand comes up to lift my chin so his eyes are in line with my own.

"You don't have to do that anymore love." He says softly stroking my cheek "You're my equal now."

I shake my head and look away from his intense eyes. Oli gives me a scared look before a short smile took his face then he hurriedly walks away.

Everyone turns away with one glare from Jayden, who is now holding me so tightly it's stopping me from breathing properly.

"Jayden," I rasp out trying to push him away, keyword: trying. His arms just encircled around me even tighter and he growls darkly. "Your suffocating me."

He instantly loosens his grip so I can step back slightly, but his super muscular arms don't give up on their hold.

"Melody." My mom's calming voice fills my ears and I instantly relax, I look to my left as she waltz over to us. Jayden doesn't move but his eyes are now on me, I can feel them burning into my head.

I don't look up and instead watch my moms silent footsteps get closer and closer. When she finally reaches us it feels like I'm 6 years older.

"Sweetie." she greets me before turning her eyes up to Jayden "Alpha."

My mom bows her head respectfully at Jayden who bows back. He stays silent but doesn't stare at me anymore, which is thankfully less nerve racking.

"Would you two care for some brunch? We're serving it in the dining room in 5 minutes. So chop chop, fill up your stomachs before you leave!" My mom says cheerfully before bouncing off.

I let out a laugh at her happy bouncing walk, she looks so weird.

"Melody." His voice is husky and deep making my heart beat faster, what is he doing to me? "Are you hungry?"

I nod and forcefully remove myself from his arms, he gives me a short annoyed growl but I just roll my eyes.

"I'm going to have food and say goodbye to the people I love." I grit out before flicking my hair behind me as I stalk away from him.

I get to the dining room and instantly take a deep breath and smile. My mom always told my brother and I 'Never leave with a frown, it's a smile that makes it mark.'

I never understood it until a few years ago, I think it's because me younger self didn't realise what it was as it didn't rhyme.

I make my way to the already crowded dining room table which was covered in food. From cheetos to pizza. From lemonade to champagne.

I skip the queue for the food as my stomach feels like throwing out food instead of taking it in. Instead I grab a beer from the end of the table.

I open it easily with the beer opener left on the table, I take a small sip and sigh. Even though it would take about triple the amount humans take to get a werewolf drunk it's nice to get the buzz.

Even a little buzz can help your mood, but sometimes it can make it worse.

I take another sip but this one turned into a large gulp instead. Before I could take another gulp a hand snatches it harshly from my hand.

I turn angrily to the person who effortlessly has taken my beer to find my father giving me a stern look. I instantly lower my head and lean against the wall.

"What are you doing El?" My father says placing the beer the other side of himself so I couldn't reach it.

"Having a beer." I say shrugging my shoulders and looking around the room. Everyone is having a great time.

There's a group of moms friends gossiping and having some champagne in one corner. In another there is a group of young teen boys all talking, some on their phones.

There are mates splattered everywhere, it felt like someone had put all the mates from the pack in here. Some were holding hands which was fine but others were snogging.

"I know your 18 but I don't like this. You've only drunk beer twice in your life, and that was never in the middle of the day while in the company of royals and the older members of the pack." My father states sounding disappointed.

"I needed something to help." I say in a whisper, not knowing if I want him to hear me or not. Against me was his werewolf hearing.

"Help with what?" He says picking up a glass of what looked like scotch from the table.

"Help with today, okay?!" I say frustrated "My so called soul mate, who I only met yesterday, is making me leave my home and all the people that I love! He hasn't seemed to care how I'm feeling about this, but I suppose that's just Alpha's isn't it! They think they own everybody! Well guess what he doesn't own me! I didn't want this! I don't have a mate remember?! It's too much in one day!" I am shouting now, and trying not to cry. I can feel the water in my eyes.

My father looks at me in sympathy but then his eyes glance behind me, his whole body stiffens and his eyes become wide.

Feeling curious, I turn around and see everyone looking at the dining room door. A small gasp left my lips as his big muscular figure blocks the doorway. His eyes show hurt and sorrow.

My wolf yearns to comfort him but I can't let myself feel bad for him. Not when he is making me change my whole life.

He walks over to me and I notice how everyone, including my father, exits the room leaving me alone with Jayden.

I avoid his eyes and look at the floor instead. I watch his feet coming closer until finally his toes are against my own, he places a thumb under my chin and lifts it up.

"You don't have a mate?" He says questioningly, I finally give in and look into his deep blue ocean pools.

I open my mouth to say something but the words are caught in my throat, the lump is making my eyes water and my emotion to become overwhelmingly sad.

"How do you explain this then?" He asks intertwining our fingers together, the electric sparks shoot up my arm making a shiver roll down my back. The smirk that finds his face is so glamorous that I smile.

I quickly get a hold of myself and shake my head in annoyance. I pull my hand from his and step away, well I try but he grabs my hand once more and pulls me back.

"Why won't you accept me? I'm your mate. I'm standing right in front of you awaiting those precious words to slip from your gracious lips." He says, the hurt in his eyes making it unbearable to look at those ocean depths.

"I-I don't have a mate..." I whisper, only half believing it myself. The mate bond between us is strong, stronger than anyone warned me about.

I can already feel it wrapping itself around the both of us and slowly pulling us together. He's given in but I haven't, yet.

My heart has acknowledged him as my mate and accepted him, the same as my wolf. On the other hand there is my brain that has acknowledged that we will both most likely die if I don't mate with him and that my heat will be coming.

But half of my brain still is convinced that I have no mate. That I, the daughter of what people call the greatest Alpha couple in centuries, am destined to be alone.

Obviously the moon Goddess has a different path she wants me to take. What if I don't want this path? What if I think this is going to quickly?

Jayden's warm hand on my cheek made me awaken from my thoughts, I can't even remember what I last said to him.

"You have a mate Melody." He says gently stepping closer, if that was even possible considering he's practically stepping on my toes.

"Melody!" My little brother Joe pops up happily from behind me. His mischievous eyes dance from me to Jayden then back to me.

I instantly take control of the matter and take a few steps away from Jayden's warmth.

"Hey little buddy!" I say ruffling his hair and flinging an arm around his shoulder in a headlock.

"Oi! El's get off me!" He winges but I hear his laughter, I let go and he gives me a playful punch on the arm. He pulls me down and whispers "Melody, why is the Alpha Prince starring at us?"

A deep red blush fills my cheeks as I glance up at Jayden who is in fact starring at us with a grin.

"Come on Jo Jo, lets go get some food!" I say rushing towards the table to grab some food, I feel his presence near me as I get in the line for food.

His scent is strong making my thoughts jumble and my mind wander. So much in fact that I accidentally try to pick up a very hot plate instead of a paper plate.

I scream in agony as I yank my hand away from the plate urgently. I shake my burning hand in attempt to cool it but it just throbs.

Jayden is by my side in a blink of an eye, fussing over me. His hands are everywhere; on my hand, arm, waist, shoulder.

I am about to finally snap at him when my Mom comes toddling along, she holds out her hand so I place mine in hers.

"Come on you nimninny." She chuckles before turning to Jayden "Alpha, your parents were searching for you. They are waiting for you on the training fields."

Jayden looks down at my indecisively, his eyes flicker to my hand then back to my eyes.

"Go," I say trying to control my quivering voice "I'll be fine."

Even though I can see that he doesn't want to go he finally gives me a curt nod and rushed out of the room stiffly. My wolf begs to stay with him but my moms pulls me into the kitchen.

She places my hand under the cold water flowing from the tap. I let out a hiss of pain but soon it vanished and my hand became numb.

Thanks to werewolf healing, it should be healed in a few minutes maybe an hour.

I could hear her lecturing me about safety and concentrating on what I'm doing, I should listen to her.

Yet all I could think about was those electric ocean pools.

CHAPTER 8

Time goes by quickly for rest of my time left here. It teases me. The clock strikes quarter to 1 and my heart drops.

The wind blows against my long hair as I sit on the bench on the back porch. I watch the people running around, laughing and training.

I smile as memories of James and I training flash across my eyes. My favourite being the day I finally beat him in a fight. He whined about it for weeks so I kept teasing him.

"Melody." My parents appear from the back door with dad smiles on their faces. I let myself smile as they sit down either side of me.

The sun is high is the sky now but the grey clouds are moving in. It's storm season here, so that means clouds and rain most days.

This is my favourite season, the wind bartering against my windows and the thunder cracking in the distance. Going for a run in the pouring rain, Keith it soak through my fur and awaken my senses.

"You okay sweetie?" My father speaks up disrupting the silence in the air.

"I-I think so." I say with a sigh "everything is changing so fast."

"I know sweetheart." My mom says giving me a hug. "I felt the same way when I met your father, I was confused."

"I know you've told me." I say trying not to roll my eyes "Bur you didn't have any parents or people; you came here to go to school so you were living with father anyways. I'm moving away. Also you knew you had a mate mom, I have never believed I do. My brain is hurting, it's all too much."

My parents look at me in sympathy and I hate it, I hate being the centre of attention of being sympathized.

"It'll be fine Melody," my father says smiling down at me "from what I've seen Jayden is a great fella, he seems to care about you and he's trying really hard for you. But your life is going to be different now. Jayden is going to be Alpha King as soon as you are mated, and you shall be Luna Queen."

Oh crap. Luna Queen! I'd forgotten about that.

"Alpha. Luna." A guard appears on the porch by the door, I instantly get to my feet and my parents follow suite. "The King and Queen request your presence along with Miss Melody; they are in the main lobby."

I look at my mom who gives me a smile and puts an arm around my shoulder; we head into the academy and follow the guard to the main lobby. I try to take my time and look around the place where I have lived my entire life but my mom's grip around my shoulder was too tight.

We arrive into the lobby in no time at all and my stomach sinks, the King and Queen stand by the opened main door talking while some guards carry their luggage into their few SUV's that are parked outside.

I let myself discretely sniff the air and to my amazement I do not smell Jayden anywhere, he must have other duties to attend to before we leave. I hate the fact that my mood dampens because he isn't here.

The King turns around and gives us a heartwarming smile, the Queen looks around and her warm inviting eyes instantly find mine.

My father shakes the King's hand and I allow my ears to tune out as they start chatting until the Queen comes out of nowhere. After jumping out of my skin I smile at the gentle woman standing in front of me.

Luna Queen Kate Beaumont is a stunning woman who doesn't look her age at all, with golden yellow hair that is pulled up tightly in a tall bun on which rests her crown. Her figure is small yet she is the same size as me, if not maybe slightly taller.

"Melody," she greets me with a warm motherly hug "it's nice to finally meet you properly. Considering last time I was watching my son chase you out of the ball room."

A deep crimson blush finds my face as we pull out of a hug; the Queen laughs at my face and rubs my arm in comfort.

"Its fine, don't be embarrassed. When I met my dear old Russell I was scared out of my mind so much so that I locked myself in a bathroom for 2 hours." She lets out a hearty laugh "That did not stop him from finding me; he ended up breaking the door down."

I can't help but allow a giggle to escape my lips as I glance at the King who is happily chatting with my father.

"I'm sorry about the running away bit." I saw awkwardly, I grasp my lip between my lip nervously as I watch the Queen's expression carefully for any signs of anger.

"Oh don't worry about it dear, you seem like a wonderful young lady and I am happy to admit that I think you are the perfect mate for my son." She says giving me yet another warm motherly hug.

"Thank you, Luna." I say bowing my head respectfully, I should say that I accept Jayden but my mind is in a battle at the moment and I don't know which side is winning yet.

"Oh please, you are to be my daughter. Call me Kate." She says giving me a heartwarming smile. "Russell, dear come meet our new family member!"

I notice the King politely dismiss himself from my father and walk over to us with a smile; his aurora makes me instantly bow my head.

"Oh no need to bow for me, you are one of us now." The King says patting my shoulder gently before putting it around his wife "Can I say it's a pleasure to welcome you in the royal castle, I know many are excited to finally meet Jayden's mate and their future Luna Queen."

"Thank you Alpha, it is an honor to be accepted." I say smiling up at them, my wolf starts moving around my head signaling that Jayden is close by. My eyes instantly start searching for him on their own will; I shake my head and mentally scold myself.

"Oh please, just call me Russell. We are family now." I smile and wonder how they have accepted me so quickly. I have only known them for like 10 minutes and they are already talking about me becoming Luna Queen.

"Melody." My mom's familiar voice floats around me making my mood instantly decrease as it hits me again, I'm leaving.

I bow to Russell and Kate before turning around, the tears fill my yes instantly as I see; my parents, 3 brothers, Victoria, James and Jesse. They all give me big smiles and I run to them straight away, they all engulf me into a large group hug.

"I love you guys so much." I sob into my mom's shoulder.

"We all love you Melody and we're going to miss you so much." My father speaks up as we all pull away from each other.

"Melody," I hear the King speak up, interrupting the family moment "The cars are all packed, we must leave I'm afraid. My wife and I are expected at the castle and we cannot be late."

I nod and suck in my tears as I turn back to my family. I hug each one of them and tell them I love them and I'll miss them, they all start crying even James and my Father.

His scent fills my nose and my whole body relaxes instantly, even if part of me wants to punch him for coming into my life and changing everything.

"Melody." His voice is a soft sigh from behind me, but his close proximity makes my whole body heat up. I turn around slowly and his arms find their way around my waist, I suck in a breath at the alien feeling.

"I'm sorry." He leans in to whisper in my ear "I didn't mean for this to happen, but you have to understand that I wouldn't be able to cope without you by my side and I can't leave my kingdom without an heir."

I nod slowly at him and smile, my wolf howls in happiness at the sparks flowing from his arms into my waist. On the other hand there is me, who is still very annoyed.

"Alpha Jayden," one of the royal guards interrupts us "The King and Queen have set off, they have given orders that you must leave immediately."

"Thank you Jacob." Jayden dismisses the guard then turns to look down at me with sad eyes. "I'm sorry love, but we must set off. I'll let you say your final goodbye; I'll wait in the car." He places a ghostly kiss on my forehead before walking away.

I turn back around to find it is only my parents left, everyone else was gone.

"They couldn't cope with saying goodbye; they'll wave from the top window." My mom says crying and giving me a smile

"As Dr Seuss said," I say "Don't cry because it's over. Smile because it happened."

————

The car journey seemed to take forever. I was sitting in the front passenger seat while Jayden is driving; his posture is stiff ad his eyes every so often would look at me.

I stayed completely still with my eyes focused on the road ahead although I watch Jayden in my peripheral vision, I literally couldn't keep my eyes off him and every time I did look at him questions would pop into my mind.

What will our life be like if I accept him? Has he ever been in a relationship before? Who is he really?

I move my feet up into the seat and wrap my arms around my knees; I lay my head on my knees and watch the trees flying past us as we speed down the long winding road.

"Love, don't be angry with me. I can't stand it." Jayden's breaks the silence. All his voice does is make me want to climb onto his lap and kiss him, stupid mate pull.

His hand removes itself from the steering wheel and finds my knee; the sparks immediately ignite as he gives me knee a soft reassuring squeeze.

"Please say something, amore mio." He pleads but my mind focuses on the fact that big wolves have now surrounded the car and are running alongside us.

"What's happening?" I ask curiously putting my legs down and sitting up. I hear Jayden let out a long sigh before answering me.

"Its border patrol making sure we're safe until we get further into the royal grounds." He explains while he refocuses on the road, his hand retreats from my knee and I can't help but feel cold without his touch.

"I think they also just want to get a glimpse of their future Luna Queen." He gives me a stupid smirk and he grabs my hand in his. My hand fits in his perfectly and I smile even if I don't want to like it, I do.

"They are most likely just happy to have their King and Queen back." I say before muttering "and their annoying ass Prince."

He growls deeply at me and his hand squeezes mine, hard.

"Don't test me, love." He says through gritted teeth "My wolf does not react well to disrespect."

"What happened to 'we are equals'?" I sneer in annoyance, if he thinks for even a minute that he can control me then he has another thing coming. I am stubborn and sarcastic so he better put on his big boy pant or I'll we are going to have problems.

He sighs and lets go of my hand, his eyes focus on the road but I can tell that they are hardened and angry.

"Awh, the big bad Alpha Prince isn't use to being fought with is he?" I say with a wicked laugh, my wolf is growling. She is begging for me to stop but my brain is in control of everything and right now it is extremely annoyed at Jayden.

His snarl echoes around the car making me freeze in my seat. His foot stomps on the brake so thank the moon goddess that I had a seat belt on. Well until Jayden reaches over and ripping my seat belt off then pulling me onto his lap.

His claws are sharp against my waist making me squirm but I don't move in fear of making him angrier. His eyes are almost pitch black now signaling his wolf and his anger.

"You don't get it, amore mio." He says with a growl in his voice before shaking his head. With a few deep breaths of my scent his eyes go back to his amazing electric blue eyes. His face lights up with a mischievous smirk.

"I am an Alpha. Tu sei il mio compagno or in english, you are my mate Melody. Yes you are my mate and yes you are my equal but this is new territory to me too. I've never been an equal with another before. So as much as you are scared, so am I okay?" He says softly caressing my cheek.

"Okay, I'm sorry." I say trying to shake off how sexy he was speaking in Italian; I wonder why he is talking in Italian. I look over him in our close proximity, his cheek bones are sharp and well cut then there is his eyes are intense but glowing an ocean blue.

I bite my lip nervously making his hungry eyes dart to my lips; I let my eyes wonder down to his delicious-looking lips. He growls lowly.

"Can I kiss you?" He whispers leaning in closer, my nerves hit the roof and my heart beat races as his lips are centimetres away from me.

In the heat of the moment I nod and he slowly places his hands on either side of my face, his lips come in contact with mine gently and the electricity ignites making butterflies erupt in my stomach.

This is going to be harder than I thought.

CHAPTER 9

His mouth is so warm, the caress of his lips softer than I could of ever imagined. He tasted tentatively with his tongue, and I allow his tongue to slip into my mouth.

His hand finds the back of my neck and pulls me in closer. His lips start to get hungrier making my senses snap, I place my hands on his chest and push him away.

His breathing is heavy alike my own. An ecstatic grin found Jayden's face making me let out a short laugh, he looks like a kid who just got a big lollypop.

A knock on the window makes me jump out of my skin and bang my head on the roof of the car. I let out a pained groan and roll off Jayden's lap onto my own seat.

Jayden growls at the man standing outside his car window then instead of seeing what the man wants, he turns to me.

"You okay?" He says grabbing my hand in a comforting manner, but my mind is still spinning from our kiss. I am also having a mental battle with myself for allowing him to kiss me.

"Um yes I think so." I say rubbing the top of my head before pointing at the man "You should see what he wants you know."

Jayden gives me an annoyed glance then rolls down the window, I look out the front car window and see wolfs scattered everywhere watching over us.

"Alpha, you are needed at the palace." The man says bowing his head. Jayden nods then the man disappears, he lets it a sigh and presses down on the gas.

"Sorry amore mio, we can get back to that later." He says with a flirty wink making me blush, I turn away from him and try to calm my ravaging heart beat.

"Can I ask you something?" I say trying to steer the conversation away from what happened moments ago.

"Of course." He says glancing at me before refocusing on the road. I look at his cute frown of concentration and giggle.

"Well I was wondering why do you speak in Italian?" I say leaning my head back against the car seat.

"Amore mio, I am from Italian heritage. My whole family is Italian born except my mother who is American. My Italian accent comes through off and on, also we speak Italian in the pack most of the time." He explains, it all makes sense now.

We make a final turn out of the forestry and I gasp loudly making Jayden laugh. He reaches over and grabs my hand, then after placing a kiss on my knuckles he says.

"Melody Wilhelm, welcome to your new home Castello Di Luna Crescente, Crescent Moon Castle ." Jayden announced proudly while I stare at the castle in front of me.

"The castle is surrounded by forest for us wolves. Yet one side of the castle, at the back, there is a large cliff drop. The back gardens falls just on the edge and it is a beautiful view." He explains as we drive through the large castle gates.

My mouth hangs open in awe at my new home. The castle looks old but so beautiful and magnificent, it's tall and the light brick work is amazing. The bright green trees surround the castle making it stand out brightly.

The towers rise above the main part of the castle and touch the clouds. The whole castle looks as though it was taken from a fairy tale.

The mountains circle the castle giving it protection and even more beauty.

"It's amazing." I breathe out, my eyes not leaving the castle once.

"Good I'm glad." Jayden replays happily "I can't wait to show you the inside!" His excited tone reminded me much of a little boy making me giggle.

I stare at the castle in complete memorization we come to a stop outside the large entrance doors. A guard opens my door and bows his head as I hop out of the big black SUV.

Jayden uses his wolf speed to rush to my side and growl at the male guard. His arm snakes around my waist and he leads me towards the large grand doors.

Stupid protective possessive mate.

Until he fully mates me then I guess I'm going to have to put up with him being possessive.

The grand doors swung open just as we were about to walk into it. My mouth once again falls open at the beauty of the inside décor.

It looks ancient yet with a modern twist to it, there is a magnificent stairway straight opposite the door and rooms branching off in every direction. I notice on the left side there is a grand double doors, miniature versions of the front main doors.

"Jayden, Melody, you're here" I hear Kate's soothing voice, I turn my head around to see her small figure walking over to Jayden and I.

I push myself out of Jayden's arms and blush as his mom walks over to me. She gives me a knowing smile as I blush beetroot red.

Jayden gives me an annoyed scowl but instead of grabbing me again he storms off to talk to a group of guards on the opposite side of the room.

I roll my eyes and turn back to Kate who is now standing in front of me, wow that little woman moves fast.

"Do you like the Castello Di Luna Crescente?" She says smiling, she must of seen my face fall at her Italian. "Hey one day I'll teach you some Italian! I mean you're going to be a Queen soon and we all use Italian."

I put on a fake smile to hide the nerves and fear swirling inside me. I start feeling dizzy and my heart beat fastens, oh no.

"Where is the bathroom please?" I ask Kate trying to keep my voice steady.

"Up the stairs then third door to your left." Kate replies before giving me a smile then wondering off and out of the room.

I race up the stairs with only one thing on my mind, I'm having a panic attack. I slam open the bathroom door then lock it once I get in.

I sit down on the closed toilet seat then my chest starts hurting, my heart starts pounding and it gets difficult to breathe properly.

I try to control it and I try to breath but my mind runs wild with thoughts of my future.

What am I going to do? I have to speak Italian, what if I don't get it? Will it ruin the pack? Will the pack hate me for it? What about Jayden? Would he reject me if I don't learn it? Would the King and Queen disapprove? How will I cope with all this new information?

A knock on the door makes me jump then my head spins and my vision starts getting blurry. "Mio amore." Jayden's voice floats into my ears making my wolf instantly calmer.

My breathing gets heavier and my chest constricts so much I wince in pain. Jayden must of heard me because he bursts through the door and speeds to my side.

His eyes wonder over me then he rubs my back gently and pulls my closer. "Deep breathes. It's alright, in and out."

I look up into his ocean blue eyes and breathe in his masculine pine scent, I immediately start calming down. My breathing evens out, my heart rate slows down and my head stops spinning.

His arm slowly finds it way around my waist and he hugs me softly. I hug him back enjoying being able to breathe properly again.

"What happened Melody?" He whispers in my ear, I snuggle into his chest and breathe in his intoxicatingly amazing smell.

"I had a panic attack." I say into his chest, making it come out muffled and incomplete.

"I realised that love," he says pulling me away from his chest to look down at my face "but why?"

"Because everything is changing so quickly! My head can't keep up!" I say feeling it build up in my chest once again "The second I walk into this gigantic castle, you leave me and your mom starts telling me about learning Italian for when I'm Queen! Do you realise how frightening that is?! The other day I was just a member of the Alpha Family and now I'm going to be the Luna Queen!"

My eyes are burning with I shed tears but I will not let them fall. I am not weak, but really I am right now.

Jayden looks me in the eye and I can see the regret and concern clear in his beautiful eyes. I love his eyes.

"I'm so so sorry, love. I know this is a lot to handle and I promise I won't leave your side again until you wish for me to leave. I understand this is all happening so fast but I can't bare to be apart from you." He says putting his head in my neck.

I lean against his chest and enjoy this moment, of us. Without my thoughts of having no mate interrupting.

"Jayden." I say against his warm muscular chest, he hums in reply "What are the sleeping arrangements?"

I blush when he looks at my face with a stupid smirk on his own. I try to punch him in the chest but he grabs my hand and kisses my knuckles.

The tingles and electricity flowing from his touch is incredibly and increasing the mate pull. I realise that we will most likely end up mating but my brain keeps going back to when I thought I had a mate and everybody else had one except me.

That was a dark time for me, filled with tears and panic attacks worse than what I just went through. My wolf and I went into depression, I would secretly go months without eating and lock myself in my bedroom for days.

"Well I guessed you probably don't want to stay in the same bed as me." He says taking my hand and gently pulling me out of the bathroom.

He walks me down a long corridor to a spiral staircase but when I looked the staircase went up as far as I can see. This castle is awesome and beautiful, and somehow it's my home too.

***

I pant in exhaustion as I exit the spiral stairs that I now hate. We just climbed 4 stories of stairs and I really was not prepared for it.

I bend over panting heavily, trying to regain my breathing. I glance at Jayden who is completely fine, he is just starring at me grinning.

I grumble some inappropriate words as I stand up, regaining my normal breathing pattern.

He growls at me. "Those words should never come out of such a beautiful mouth." He says running his thumb over my bottom lip.

Ignoring the pull to kiss him I push him away from me "I can say what I like." I say "Now show me my room please."

My face stays straight but inside is a fight, between my brain, my heart and my wolf. Also the mate pull which is getting stronger and harder to ignore.

"Of course." He says with a mock bow before taking both my hands and walking in front of me.

I laugh as he tries not to trip, his face is frowning in concentration so I pull him to a stop. He looks at me with a embarrassed smile, I reach up and run my finger over his frowning forehead.

He reaches over and cups my face in his large hands, I move my hands to grip his wrists as my eyes focus on his.

"Melody," His voice is a whisper as he leans in closer "My beta is calling me." It comes out in an angry growl, obviously that isn't what he planned to happen. He drops his hands from my face and I blush.

"Why? Do you have to go?" I say trying to not let the sadness appear in my voice. He grabs my hand and places a gentle kiss on my knuckles.

"He needs me to do some paper work," He smirks at me "and I have to sort out your Luna files and paperwork."

I smile but my stomach drops, I still don't know how I feel about this.

"Okay." I whisper looking at my feet "uh where should I wait until.. .erm you get back? I don't know where anything is or even where my room is."

Jayden walks back the way we came a few steps, his eyes are glazed over signalling that he is talking to someone on mind link.

I watch him carefully as he stands still, his muscles are bulging through his thin white t-shirt and the one thing I can't get out of my mind is his lips.

The lips I kissed not even an hour ago and now all I want to do is kiss him again. Suddenly I feel like my body is working without me behind the steering wheel.

I find myself in front of him in a second flat, my hand reaches up and touches his cheek which instantly makes his eyes turn back to their electric blue.

He looks down at me and before he can say anything I go on my tip toe and press my lips to his.

CHAPTER 10

At first he doesn't respond so I move to pull away, feeling rejected. Then suddenly his hands grip my waist and pull me back.

I instinctively wrap my arms around his neck as he kisses me back with so much power I feel like he is going to knock me backwards.

His hands are moving under my top now and I can feel how excited he is getting. My nerves skyrocket making me push his away quickly, that was getting out of hand.

Get a hold of yourself, Melody!

He beams and holds me at arms length. "I must admit mio amore, your an excellent kisser." He says with a wink.

I punch his arm half in anger half in playfulness. I need some time to myself, to think about whats going on and how to control this.

"So when do you have to go?" I ask moving myself to the other side of the corridor to lean on the wall. The wall is cold, cooling down my heated body.

"Now." He sighs "Your personal body guards, Tate and Derek will be here any second now though. So just wait here and they shall be here the second I'm gone."

He starts walking down the corridor in a fast walk, when he gets to the top of the stairs he turns to me with a pained expression.

"Don't do anything stupid or reckless." He says, finally with our distance my thought start clearing. I roll my eyes and let out a huff.

He disappears down the stairs and not even two seconds later two bulky men appear. I jump in surprise, werewolf speed always amazes me.

"Luna." The chorus and bow at me, I scowl darkly at them. Even though my wolf is bouncing with happiness at the respect she is getting for being Luna.

"Please refrain from calling me Luna, that is not my name. My name is Melody so please use it!" I say reaching out to shake both of their hands.

"Well I'm Tate!" The tallest of the two speaks up. He has bleach blonde hair and brown hazelnut eyes, he is muscular and looks like he could get as many girls as he liked. Although he is tall, he is not as tall as Jayden.

"I'm Derek." The other guy speaks up, he seems a lot more quieter than Tate. Unlike Tate, he has pitch black hair and purplish eyes. From what I can smell, he is mated.

"So," I say shifting my feet across the wooden floor "what shall we do now?"

"We were instructed to keep an eye on you wherever you go." Derek says, making me growl mentally. Honestly Jayden actually thinks I'm going to be followed every where 24/7.

If I should believe Jayden to be my mate and give my heart and soul to him I will not become the stereotypical mate. I am not weak so I do not need to be followed everywhere.

He can go put his head down the toilet if he thinks I'm going through with this. And if he thinks that I'm not going to be reckless, well he should of thought about that before ripping me away from my family.

"Yes I realised that." I say trying to not let the annoyance in my voice slip through "but what can we do? Instead of standing in this deserted corridor like weirdos."

"Well we could go to the Alpha Prince's game room." Tate smirks giving me a nudge with his shoulder "because I know the Luna, who is the only other person beside the Alpha who is allowed in there, wants to play FIFA."

He tries to wink at me. I laugh at his face, this boy cannot wink to save his life. It's coming out as normal blinking and making him look very unattractive.

"That sound like fun!" I say "lets do it!"

***

"How the heck are you so good?!" Tate groans in annoyance as I get past his goalie and score yet another goal.

"Well living with 3 brothers opens ones eyes to Xbox games!" I laugh leaning back against the sofa and passing the controller back to Derek, who has come out of his shell in the past hour.

I haven't heard from Jayden since he left but Derek told me he was busier than he thought he would be. Yet while we are apart I finally get to think clearly, and I've come to the my senses.

I did not want to come here, but I reluctantly agreed. Then as soon as we arrive he leaves me alone most of he afternoon and evening.

Yet he's checking up on me every five minutes. I'm already losing my mind and patience.

I've have, however, enjoyed being with Tate and Derek. I found out, in an hour, that Derek has 2 older sisters and has a mate who works as one of the top Pack Doctors. He has also invited me to have dinner with them once I'm settled.

Then there is Tate who is the typical male wolf, wants his mate badly but won't admit it because he is too cool. He told me he broke up with his long term girlfriend about a month ago because she found her mate, this made him finally decide to wait for his mate.

"Guys." I say breaking free of my trance, they both him in reply but concentrate on the game. "Has Jayden ever been with someone?"

They both freeze instantly, this makes my heart speed up. My nerves sky rocket and I mentally curse this stupid mate bond.

"FIFA is boring now." Tate exclaims turning the xbox off "How about we raid the Alpha's kitchen?"

"As much as I love that idea." I say with a long sigh, am I really doing this to myself? "Be honest with me about Jayden, please."

"He hasn't been with anyone in a serious way but he is not a virgin." Derek says lightly "now lets raid the kitchen."

I slowly nod and stand up. So Jayden didn't wait, even though he is all for mates. Whereas I was anti-mate yet I still saved myself for the one I would fall for.

I can't control the sadness that washes over me like a wave. My wolf is crying because her mate did not save himself for her which is what you're suppose to do.

I nod to the guys then follow them to Jayden's private kitchen, it's only for me and him. I found out that on the 4th floor at the very side of the castle is mine and Jayden's side.

"What do you guys want?" I ask looking in the giant fridge. The kitchen is all dark wood and marble, it has an island in the middle and two full fridges.

"I don't mind as long as it's awesome!" Tate says fist bumping the air.

I laugh and grab the ingredients for the only things I know how to make, pancakes!

After I grab the ingredients from the fridge, I get a bowl and mix them together. Tate and Derek sit quietly watching me.

"Jayden will be back soon." Derek breaks the silence, I look at him and nod slowly. I thought I'd have more time to think without him messing with my mind.

I glance at the clock hanging from the wall, it's just gone 10pm. I don't reply to Derek, not knowing what to say. The atmosphere quickly becomes silent and tense.

"Does the whole pack know about me?" I ask flipping the second pancake onto a plate. I turn back and pour more mixture into the pan, I can feel Derek and Tate's eyes on me but I keep my back to them.

"Well yes, basically the whole pack know that Jayden has found his mate. But apart from the wolves on the territory line and some people in the castle, nobody knows your identity." Tate says leaning back in the island chair he is occupying.

"Oh right, okay." I say with a nod, I finish up with the pancakes quickly and give them to the boys. They eat them all in minutes, I let out a long unattractive laugh at their piggish eating style.

"Aren't you having any?" Derek asks pushing his empty plate away from him. Tate burbs loudly and pushes the plate towards me.

"No." I shake my hand grabbing the two plates and putting them in the sink. "I'm not hungry."

"I think you should eat Melody." Tate says looking serious for the first time since I met him "You haven't eaten all day and Jayden will have our heads if he knew that."

"I'm fine, thanks for you concern though. Plus Jayden doesn't need to know." I shrug, truth is I didn't even realise that I haven't eaten all day.

"What doesn't Jayden need to know?" I freeze in my spot as his scent fills me up and his questioning voice startles me.

I turn around to see him standing threateningly in the doorway of the kitchen. His cold eyes are starting daggers at the two men who have been my company for the past few hours.

"Jayden doesn't need to know anything because it's rude to listen to a conversation you're not involved in." I say in annoyance while glaring at him.

He glances at me for a second before turning back to the guys, "you may leave."

I roll my eyes and turn to the sink, I wash the plates slowly as I hear the heavy footprints of the guys running out of the room.

Arms wrap around my waist startling me, Jayden buries his face into my neck and sighs. His warm breath fans my sweet spot and I have to bite back a moan.

"What's wrong?" He whispers sweetly, it's so strange how his personality changes from when he is Alpha to when he is with me.

"I'm tired." I say, I turn around in his hold and look up at him "can you just tell me where my room is so I can sleep?"

"Of course, it's three doors down right at the end of the corridor. You're right opposite my room as well in case you need me." He says resting his forehead against mine instead of in he crook of my neck.

"Okay thanks." I say, holding back a yawn. The exhaustion washes over me making me crave a nice warm bed.

"Oh also, I have good news!" Jayden says excitedly "I've filled out all your Luna Queen paperwork! And my parents are arranging the party to introduce you to everyone!"

I stare at him with my mouth hanging open, is he serious? I only just got here-I was forced to come here as well- and now he wants me to meet the pack! And he's done my Luna Queen paperwork when we haven't even mated yet!

Anger quickly replaces my shock, I shove his chest hard making him stumble away from me. He growls in annoyance so I growl back even louder.

"What the heck are you thinking?!" I scream "I only arrive here hours ago, and not by my own choosing either! You disappeared leaving me in a strange place with people I had never met before! Then you come back in saying I'm meeting the pack and you've filled my Luna paperwork! You never asked me about this! You never asked if I was okay with this! No you only care about yourself Jayden! That's why you stole me away from my home only to leave me alone to do work!"

I storm out of the kitchen and find my room in seconds using my wolf speed. I slam the door as loud as I can before locking it to make sure he can't get it.

Not even a second after I twist the lock Jayden is outside the door, knocking.

"Love, I'm sorry okay? Please let me in. Let's talk about this. I'm sorry, you don't have to do anything you don't want to. I promise." He says gently through the door.

I lean against the wall and slide to the floor. A traitor tear falls down my cheek and onto the floor.

I don't want to be here.

CHAPTER 11

4 hours later...

I wake up in a cold sweat, my heart is racing and my head is pounding. I clutch my head as my mind swirls at the nightmare that I just witnessed.

I can't even remember it now I have awakened, but all I know is it was scary and the fresh tears of my face can prove that. Thunder bangs making me jump.

I look out the window and see the rain bartering against the window. The darkness outside makes the lightning brighten up the room. I love storm season.

I run my hands down my face and try to remember the dream, but it was irretrievable. My wolf cries out for the comfort of her mate in our alarmed state.

I glance towards the door and can hear his heartbeat coming from the room across the hall. Should I go over there?

Another crack of thunder bursts from outside, I instantly jump from my bed. I pad my way out of my bedroom and find myself at Jayden's door.

Do I knock?

My confusion spirals in my mind. I lift my hand to knock then stop, what if he is asleep? I haven't even spoken to him since lock-in myself in my room last night.

I finally decide to just sneak in, it'll save me from having to explain my lost nightmare. I turn the doorknob silently and push it open, I glance in and see Jayden fast asleep on his bed.

He looks so peaceful, his hair is dishevelled and his mouth is slightly open. My eyes can't help but notice that he is shirtless and the thin comforter has fallen to his waist.

Ignoring my wolfs begs to join him, I make my way to the sofa in the corner of the room after shutting the door quietly.

I love the two cushions to one side and lay my head on them. I don't have a blanket so instead I curl into a ball. I close my eyes and breathe in Jayden's scent.

Just as I feel myself surrendering to sleep, a very sleepy husky voice wakes me up.

"Melody?" He asks in confusion as he sits up then turns on the lamp next to his bed. I wince at the brightness.

Another crack of lightning brightens the room, illuminating his gorgeous abs and face. I sigh and slowly sit up.

"What are you doing?" He asks, one second he is on his bed and the next he is crouching in front of me "is something wrong?"

I look into his sleepy ocean eyes trying to figure out how I'm already harbouring feelings for him. His hand reaches up and rests on my cheek.

"Melody please answer." He begs with worry evident in his voice now.

"I got scared." I whisper although I know it made no difference to whether he would hear me or not.

"What scared you, love?" He asks moving impossibly close, I grip his hand in mine feeling the need for his comfort.

"I-I can't remember." I stutter, trying to figure out what frightened me so deeply. Then again I've always been a person with many hidden fears, it's most likely to do with the fact that Jayden wants me to meet thousands of people as future Luna Queen.

That frightens me, a lot.

"Come on, you can sleep in my bed." He says "I'll take the sofa."

I hesitantly nod, he pulls me up from my spot in the couch and pulls me over to the bed. I lay down then he throws the comfort of over my body, he leans down and places a chaste kiss on my forehead.

I watch him walk to his closet and grab an extra blanket then he lays down on the sofa, which surprisingly was big enough for him.

"Jayden." I whisper into the silent darkness, I hear his hum in reply "Thank you."

"Anything for you, my love. Always." He says and not long after I hear his laboured breathing. I curl up into his blanket, his scent fills me up and Somnus soon finds me.

***

It's been 4 days since I crept into Jayden's room, and he hasn't allowed me to return to my own bed incase I have another nightmare yet my nightmare still alludes me.

Jayden and I have been growing closer making it impossible to give him the silent treatment. My wolf begs everyday to mate with him, but I'm still not sure.

Everyday I'm with Jayden he asks when or if I'll ever be ready. So far I've done a good job of changing the subject but Jayden's annoyance is growing each day.

I lay on his bed in a pair of joggers and a hoodie I stole from Jayden. I don't have any clothes here yet so I have to keep borrowing from female pack members.

I try to avoid it by wearing Jayden's clothes yet I know that he doesn't mind in the slightest. The rain outside is battering against the window has been since the early hours of the morning.

The room is still in darkness as it is still the early hours of the morning. Jayden sleeps peacefully on the sofa opposite the bed.

His bare chest shines in the moonlight as the comforter is down below his waist. His face is peaceful and his mouth is slightly open as he breathes gently.

I watch him silently thinking about how he is my mate and one day, if I am ever ready, he will be sleeping beside me as my King and my official marked mate.

I close my eyes and take a deep breath. I allow Somnus to try and find me but instead hunger creeps up on me.

I sigh in defeat then throw the blanket off my heated body. I quietly tiptoe out of the room and down the hall to Jayden's private kitchen.

I open the fridge and glance through it, allowing the ideas of different meals I could make.

"Where is the bread?" I whisper to myself, wanting to fulfil the craving for a chicken sandwich. I rummage through the fridge, the light in the fridge is the only light provided in the dark kitchen.

After failing to find any in Jayden's overloaded fridge, I make my way around the castle to the pack kitchen where I knew there would be some bread for my sandwich.

I feel the need for Jayden in my chest growing the further I get from him. My wolf is begging not to leave his side but I ignore her, I just need a sandwich.

As soon as I get to the kitchen I turn the light on then head straight to the fridge. The castle is relatively quiet except for a few guards chatting nearby.

I grab the bread, chicken and lettuce from the giant fridge. Finally. I keep quiet as I butter the bread and start piling on the chicken.

Before I can put the last piece of bread on top to complete my sandwich. A hand grabs my waist, by the itching feeling it creates I know it isn't Jayden.

Panic builds in my chest as the hand spins my around. Before I can hit the person, they grab my hands and pin them behind my back.

I look up and see a man, he is tall and muscular but his eyes have mischievous and dangerous glint to them.

"Wha-" I try to speak but he is speedy to interrupt me.

"Now now, who have we here." He taunts "a new female in the pack. Well well well. Maybe I should show you how I welcome new females."

His hand slides up my top and cups my breast, my wolf is snarling angrily in my head and all I want is Jayden. I open my mouth to scream but instead the man puts a hand over my mouth.

He has put my hands behind my back and pushed me against the counter so they are immobilised. I wince in pain as the sharp counter edge digs into my wrist.

"Now now, we don't want to scream unless your screaming my name." He says next to my ear then he places a kiss on my neck.

I squirm and the tears are falling from my face, my skin is burning at his touch and the fear is strong on my stomach making me want to throw up.

His hand moves to cup my breast fully and the tears are now gushing onto the ground. What do I do?

His hand that covers my mouth moves away so I decide to take the chance to say something.

"I'm the-" I start but he stops me once again before I can explain.

"No more talking." He says leaning in closer to my lips, I can feel his breath on my face and it sends a shiver of disgust down my spine.

Oh no. He is getting closer, I don't want him near me. I don't want anyone you touching me like this but Jayden, oh crap does that mean I'm accepting Jayden?

I whimper as his lips are almost on mine, my eyes have run out of tears and my body has resulted in body shaking sobbing.

I try and turn my head away but his hand grips my chin harshly, holding me in place as his lips are nearly on my lips.

Just before they land on my own lips a terrifying earth-shattering growl shook the entire castle. The guy in front of me whips around as a familiar comforting scent hits my nose.

Jayden.

I sigh in relief and then to face him, he stands threateningly in the doorway. His eyes are black and his claws are extending, even if deep down I know he won't hurt me I can't help but feel scared.

I'm a second he rushes to the guy and throws him across the room. I let out a scream as he hits the wall on the opposite wall, the guy falls to the floor unconscious.

I'm guessing Jayden mind-links some guards because the next minute two guards whiz in and take the guy away. I watch them then slowly turn to Jayden.

His pitch black eyes are staring at me, they scan up and down my body most likely to check if I'm injured. Then he grabs my wrist, which is sore from the sharp counter edge.

In a second he picks me up bridal style the next minute we are in his bedroom. He puts me down and starts pacing the room.

The growls emitting from him are low and dangerous, I stand still not knowing what to do. I let out a small sigh, feeling relieved that nothing to serious happened.

I can still feel his touch on my skin and it makes bile try to come up. I swallow it down and lift my hand to wipe my wet cheeks from crying.

Jayden's head snaps towards me and I can see in his eyes that he has lost control to his wolf. My heart beats faster and I look at him carefully.

Suddenly he marches over to me and puts his head in my neck. I don't know what else to do so I put my arms around his neck and just enjoy having his touch on me.

I feel him press a kiss on my soft spot making a moan rip out of my throats and my legs turn to jelly. I feel him smirk against my neck, even though he is out of control I can't help but feel safe in his arms.

I feel a sharp prick against my neck and my stomach instantly flips. He is trying to mark me, crap! I try to push him off me but his hands rip my hips tightly. His wolf is too strong.

"Jayden-" before I can continue his canines puncture deep into my skin. Black dots cloud my vision as I let out a blood curdling scream.

CHAPTER 12

After a few minutes which feel like days, Jayden pull his canines out and licks his newly made mark.

He pulls away and looks at me in the eye. The edges of my eyes are still blacked out and the tears have once again started tumble from my eyes.

The blackness in his eyes melts away into his beautiful ocean pools. He looks at me in shock then I see regret build up in his eyes.

"Crap! Melody, I-I am so sorry." He says just as my legs finally collapse, he catches me instantly and lays me on the bed. I sob into his chest while he rubs my back soothingly.

"I couldn't control him." Jayden says sounding surprised and sorrowful. "I just saw that guy touching you and trying to kiss you and lost it."

I don't reply to him because I don't trust myself right now. I feel like my emotions have turned into a swirling tornado in my mind.

All I know is I want Jayden. Now that he has marked me as his it will be almost impossible to reject our mating bond. Although I have started to slowly accept him.

After a few more hours of crying and Jayden apologising I finally stop my tears. The clock on the bedside table reads 6:58am.

I look up at Jayden who is staring at the opposite wall in deep though, his arms are tightly wrapped around my waist while his fingers draw soothing circles on my hip.

I move slightly in his hold making his eyes move from the wall to me. Seeing that I am not crying he instantly sits up and looks me in the eye.

"How are you feeling?" He asks still gripping me around the waist, but I don't mind. I just want to be near him for now and not just because of the mark, but also because I want to get the other guy out of my mind.

Only Jayden can provide the comfort and protection I am craving.

"I'm okay, I think." I say sheepishly leaning my forehead against the hot skin of his shoulder. My mind is spinning and my neck is still burning.

"Do you have to go?" My heart drops as I ask but my wolf is begging for him to stay by my side after being marked. She is so happy that it's giving me a headache. I smile as Jayden shakes his head.

"No, I've asked for the day off to stay with you. Since I - uh - marked you last night, the pack understands that I want to be with you." He explains scratching the back of his neck.

Part of me wishes to tell him that I forgive him for marking me and that it will all turn out alright. Yet the other part of me is angry at him for marking me without my consent.

Instead I stay quiet and stay leaning against him. He doesn't seem to mind, as I am now marked Jayden and I now have a mind-link but we cannot tell each other's emotions until we mate. We can only communicate.

"Oh by the way, your Doctor wants a meeting with you and I later on today." Jayden speaks up, slicing through the silence.

I frown and lean back to lookup at his face. He gives me a soft smile and rubs my back gently, making me want to purr.

"My doctor?" I question in confusion.

"Yes, the best doctor in the land. I've ordered for him to be your doctor because if anything happens to you I want you in the best hands going." He says pecking my lips softly.

I mentally awe then move away to look up at him, he looks at me intensely. He leans down and connects our lips together.

Fireworks explode in my stomach as our lips move perfectly against each other. I move to kneel in between his legs and wrap my arms around his neck.

His arms snake around my waist and he pulls me impossibly closer, he bites my lips asking for entrance which I gladly allow.

I eventually start feeling it of breath and he must of noticed because he pulls away, he leans his forehead against mine as we try to regain our breathing.

"So what do you want to do today?" He asks and I smirk up at him.

***

We ended up spending the whole day drifting in as out of sleep. Well I slept in between crying and shouting.

Jayden stayed by my side silently, rubbing my back and pulling me back into bed.

He seemed distant an it only worsened as I got better. By the end of the day he wouldn't even touch me.

It is now the morning after, Jayden had disappeared from the room and by his scent he has been gone for a while.

I let a sigh escape my mouth and echo around the room. I am still laying in Jayden's bed, being marked had exhausted me.

I rub my slightly bruised forearm gently, I woke up from a pain in my forearm and when I looked down it was bruised.

Not just the mark but the emotional rollercoaster that joined it. I spent most of yesterday crying or screaming at Jayden for marking me.

A burst of sudden white light broke the darkness in the room. The buzzing drifted into my ears making them ring slightly at the high volume.

I glance at my phone that lays on the floor by the bed, wait! I thought Jayden had taken my phone.

He explained that he didn't want anyone disturbing us or trying to convince me to leave. I quickly reach down and answer it.

"Hello." I say sounding groggy, when did Jayden leave my phone here? I sit up and stretch my back then hear a satisfying click. I sigh in relief.

"Hey sweetie!" My mom's sweet voice echoes from the other end of the phone. I instantly stand up in my excitement, this is the first time I've spoken to my mom since leaving home.

"Mom!" In shout in happiness and can't help but jump up and down. "How are you?"

"I'm okay thanks sweetie just missing my little girl!" Her voice breaks slightly, my heart sinks as I hear it. I want my mom.

"I'm missing you too mom!" I say sitting down on the edge of the bed, tears threaten to fall and because of my emotional stare they start to fall.

"How's Jayden treating you?" She asks curiously and I instantly want to tell her all about him marking me by force then leaving me.

I don't.

"It's all good! He is always with me and always helping me out." I say then take a deep breath "he marked me yesterday."

I hear my mom's voice hitch, the silence down the line is deafening and I feel my stomach flip with nerves.

"Congratulations." She says regaining her happy tone "Thats great news!"

"Yeah." I say bluntly feeling the pain in my chest at the though, I wish it was great news.

"Are you happy there sweetheart?" Mom says sounding concerned, I wish to tell the truth and for once my wolfs agrees.

My wolf loves our mom and knows we can trust and confide in her, my wolf is feeling the same way I am. Hurt. As our mate forcefully marked us and then left us alone.

"Yes! Of course!" I say trying to sound as positive as I can "The castle is huge and everybody is so lovely."

"Okay, as long as your happy then I'm happy." She says in her sweet motherly voice, I instantly just want a hug from her.

I hear a short loud knock on the door and the sadness creeps into my chest once more. I'll have to say goodbye, again.

Who knows when I'll be able to talk to my mom again. Jayden may take my phone again. What if I never get to talk to them again?

"Melody?" My mom's voice breaks me from my horrifying thoughts.

"Oh yes. Mom I have to go," I say "but I'll call you again soon!"

"Okay, I love you sweetheart." She says and more tears fall from my eyes.

"I love you mom."

The line went dead.

I take a deep breath, throw my phone back on the floor and wipe the tears from my cheeks.

I steadily got up off the bed and opened the door. Tate and Derek stood threatening and tall in the door way.

They look me up and down them storm into the room. I frown but keep quiet because I don't trust my voice.

"Sorry Lu-Melody, we saw you crying and thought someone was in here." Derek apologies and bows his head at me.

"It's okay." I reply pulling at the hem of the t-shirt I am wearing that I stole from Jayden. It's the only thing that's comforting me today, considering Jayden isn't here.

"So why were you crying?" Tate asks sitting on the sofa, then Derek falls onto the sofa next to him.

"If I tell you something do you guys have to tell Jayden?" I ask sitting down on the bed and crossing my legs. I look at the boys as they exchange glances before looking back to me with curiosity written on their faces.

"That depends." Derek replies "If you tell us something that could harm you or let you leave the castle, then yes."

"Oh." I sigh "well I'll tell you anyway, it's not like I have anyone else to talk too. I was on the phone to my parents, they want me to go home. To visit at least."

Derek and Tate look at each other and frown, they slowly turn their attention back to me and shake their heads.

"That doesn't seem likely, Jayden had told everyone to make sure you don't leave the castle. He is only letting you out there if you're with him or fully mated with him." Tate says leaning back casually.

I groan and fall back onto the bed, why did I have to be mated to the Alpha Prince! And a protective possessive one too. Just when I was finally getting use to not believing in my mate.

"Where is Jay?" I ask leaning back on my elbows so I can see them. Tate looks as though he is about to pass out from exhaustion whereas Derek looks quite awake and calm.

"He is doing some work with his father." Derek says but his eyes tell me he isn't quite telling the truth "He will be strung up all day so you won't see him."

"Oh alright then." I say standing up "Now if you fellas don't mind, I'm going to shower so get out. Please."

They both squirm and leave the room but not before they've given me a high five. They shut the door but I can feel their presence on the other side.

Oh wait, I'm marked now. I have now got a mind link with Jayden, I open the mind link and try to contact him.

'Jayden.' I say, my voice soft with uncertainty. I can feel him on the other side, my wolf can sense his wolf too.

'Yes? Is something wrong? Are you okay?' He replies instantly, I can hear the worry in his voice.

'I'm fine, where are you?' I ask, considering I was only marked yesterday I still need Jayden. And I'm starting to want him as well as need him.

'I'm out with my father, I'm busy. Only mind link me if you're hurt or in danger.' He says then disappears.

I can't help the pain that hits me in the chest, I hate this. This is why I didn't want a mate and decided I didn't have one, I didn't want this pain.

The pain of rejection. The pain of ignoring. The pain of loneliness.

I let the tears fall down to their death on the floor while I walk towards bathroom for my much needed shower.

CHAPTER 13

Time is the master of all. It controls everything. How long we live. How long our food is in the oven. How long we are in love.

Time can go by in a flash. Time can drag on forever. Time can corrupt ones very soul.

Tick tock.Tick tock.Tick tock.

I stare at the clock feeling the familiar feeling of anger and annoyance bubbling in the pit of my stomach.

I know what I have to do, but I know I'm going to get in big trouble for it. Jayden will be furious. And hurt.

It's been 3 days since I last saw Jayden, so far he has been leaving before I wake up and coming home after I've fallen asleep.

I'm deeply hurt, my wolf feels rejected that he doesn't want to be with us especially after marking us. He has blocked off his mind link completely now, he opens it regularly every so often to check on me.

I've reached the limit now, I can't cope with my wolfs constant whining and my constant chest pain. This is exactly what problems come with a mate, that I frankly didn't want.

I pace the room with my mind reeling over my stupid idea, but I know it'll finally get Jayden's attention.

This is crazy. You're gonna kill yourself.

I groan in annoyance. I have to do this because I can't get hold of him any other way, he has ordered Tate and Derek to stay with me at all times and not allow me to go near him while he is 'working'.

I know he isn't because Tate slipped up the other day and told me he was avoiding me. How was I suppose to try and fix things if he won't let me see him?!

I'm finally starting to admit to myself of the feelings I harbour for him, but it's hard when all I'm starting to feel is anger towards him.

I glance at the open window and step towards it slowly, the gusting breeze bangs the windows against the wall making me jump.

Yet another storm is rolling in so I better do this before the rain starts, I do not want to get hypothermia.

I listen carefully to the activity outside the bathroom door, I hear Tate and Derek steady heart beats from the other side of the door.

I have to be quiet.

I look out the window to see if it is clear which luckily it is, I carefully climb up onto the window frame and perch. I look down and have to gulp down my fear.

It's a 3 story drop from this window to the ground, if I'm lucky I could land with only minor bruising but if something goes wrong I could possibly die.

This is for Jayden and I.

This is stupid.

No, no it's not. Just do it!

I take a deep breath before letting my body fall off the window frame and into the hair. My heartbeat speeds up dramatically as I fall to the ground at a frightening speed.

Within seconds my feet touch the ground, I cry out in pain as my ankle cracks from the harsh contact. I use the tuck and roll move I was taught in training.

I sit there for a second trying to control the raging pain in my ankle, I glance down and see the bruising already starting. I get up as quickly as I can.

I race straight towards the forest, just as I enter the darkened tree line I hear Derek's familiar voice shout my name, "Melody!"

I ignore him but mentally smile, I keep running deeper into the woods. I can sense Jayden in my mind but keep him blocked out. They must of told him.

I get deep into the forest, I'm close to the border now so if I go further the patrol will find me. That is not what I want. I quickly, without thinking, shift into my wolf.

I stop and listen carefully. I hear the howls of wolfs, most likely signalling that I have disappeared. I pant heavily, I freeze as an unknown sound bounces off the trees around me.

It's the sound of a bear. My ears are up and I lift my head as high as I can and look around. My eyes scan my surroundings slowly as another sound reaches my ears, a wild boar.

Then another and another. I let myself growl lowly and crouch down readying myself. Instead of something coming from where the sounds are, I hear Jayden's orders from close by.

I start running towards the right instead, ignoring the random sounds I just heard. I must keep up with the plan.

The pain in my ankle is becoming almost bearable. Suddenly the ground shakes beneath my feet as a loud frightening growl bounces off the trees.

Jayden.

He's angry. I can sense it, he is completely raging. My wolf is yapping happily and the thought of finally seeing her mate.

10...

I sense his wolf getting closer making my heart thump in my chest.

9....

Will he be really angry? Will he hurt me? What if he decides to punish me?

8....

What if I can't fix this now?

7....

Have I messed this whole thing up?

6....

Will he reject me for disobeying him?

5...

His footsteps are getting closer and I can hear his angry growls.

4...

My ears prick up as I hear the twigs snapping under my feet, the pain in my ankle is forgotten as my worry about Jayden takes over.

3...

He is slowly breaking down the wall in my mind.

2...

I'm starting to feel weak and I'm giving in.

1...

His wolf comes into view and I see the anger and hurt in his pitch black eyes. I want the blue ocean pools back now.

0...

He gets ahead of me and jumps in front of me, I force myself to halt being I still crashed into him. Unlike me he kept his foot in and stood tall in front of me.

I wince as I feel my ankle starting to throb at the sudden pressure of halting. His face morphs into one of worry but it passes and the anger continues.

He breaks through the wall I put up in my head and the growl that comes through is frightening making my head spin.

'Shift now Melody.' He snarls angrily through our mind link. I bow my head but don't shift, he steps forward threateningly.

A man appears out of nowhere and chucks some short and a t-shirt at Jayden who catches them in his jaw easily. I watch as the man nods at me before racing off once again.

He shifts in front of me, I turn my head away feeling the usual shyness overcome me. He pulls on the shorts and throws the t-shirt at me.

I look at the shirt then up at him, he crosses his arms making his muscles bulge but makes no attempt to move. I quickly shift and pull on the shirt.

I stand up straight and looks at him, his eyes are still black but they look even angrier now, if that's even possible.

Without talking he grabs me then picks me up, one of his hands behind my knees and the other strongly wrapped against my back.

I sit in his arms silently, avoiding his gaze and those of strangers. I'm guessing that he told most that I escaped so the heat rises up my neck.

Jayden is using his alpha wolf speed so everything becomes blurred, I know where he is going though. His bedroom. The Alpha Prince's quarters.

Alpha Prince.

Those two words still make my head spin, because I'm mated to him. I look up to see his sharp chin which is covered in stubble.

I want to reach up and touch it. Touch him. Just to feel the comfort and sparks that come with his touch, to know we are mates.

It keeps me sane, my brain is still trying to persuade me I don't have a mate and it makes my mind a whirlwind. I'm sick of it.

I think I am ready to accept him. What harm can that do? I'll finally have a mate. Someone who will love me. Someone who will protect me.

Sooner than I realise we are in his bedroom and he throws me rather roughly onto his bed. He stands at the foot of the bed breathing extremely heavily.

His eyes are switching between black and the blue I love so much. I slowly get off my back and turn so I kneel in front of him. His eyes follow my every movement.

"Jayden-" I start but he cuts my off by roughly pushing forward and putting his lips against mine. I could tell he wanted dominance so I gave it to him, the kiss was rough and deep.

His tongue easily slips into my mouth and my hands find their way into his hair. His arms snake around my waist and he hoists me up slightly.

He pulls away and I breathe deeply trying to control myself. He rests his head against mine then, after a few peaceful seconds, he sighs loudly.

"You ran." He states painfully, his arms leave my waist and he steps away from me. He takes all positivity with him because all I feel is nervous and scared.

"I-" Jayden's eyes go darker as he glares at me, I shut my mouth instantly and look down at my lap.

"You ran from me." He states again but this time with anger "You ran from your own mate! Why Melody why?! Have I not done enough for you?!"

I try to speak but I feel as though there is a plug on my throat, stopping the words from escaping. I hear him step closer and my head tilts up to him.

"Speak." He demands.

"I ran." I say, the shock on his face is evident as he steps away from me. "But not for the reasons you believe."

He regains his composure and looks me straight in the eye. "Why did you run then Melody?"

"Because..." I run out of words because it finally hits me, even though my plan worked it was a stupid plan.

"Because what?!" He shouts this time, I flinch back in surprise. Suddenly I feel something in my stomach, it's burning and I know that's it's anger. He has finally gotten me angry.

"Because you left me!" I shout standing up off the bed "Because you were a coward who ran away the moment things got serious! You marked me, without consent may I add, then left!"

He isn't trying to hide his shock now, it's clear in his face. He looks at me before stepping forward. "Melody I-"

"No Jayden! Don't make any excuses! I don't want excuses! I don't want you to leave me! I want you with me." The anger cooks and I look up at his concentrating face.

"I-" I cut him off again.

"Jayden. I forgave you for marking me, days ago but you have avoided me. I've slept in your bed, not mine because I thought that would mean something to you but it didn't. So I ran, to get your attention. Because Jayden I...I accept you as my mate." I say.

Jayden's face morphs from anger to surprise to absolute glee. His lips tug up into a grin and he comes over to me. In seconds he places his lips on mine again, but this time the kiss is soft and slow.

He pushes me back slowly making me fall onto the bed with him on top. He keeps the kiss going but I can feel myself getting breathless, I pull away slowly.

He places kisses down my neck before surprising me with a open mouth kiss on my mark. A moan rips out of my throats and I feel my stomach flip at the sensation racing through my body.

"Melody." He says, I can hear the smirk in his voice "My Queen."

CHAPTER 14

Bliss. Absolute Bliss. That's what I'm feeling. In the arms of my over-the-moon mate after finally accepting him.

The wave of ecstatic happiness rolls of Jayden as he curls me deep into him. He is staring down at me while playing with a strand of my hair.

I wonder what's going through his head at this very moment. I know that in my head I have thoughts of our future, I can't help them following through my brain. I know he's happy but does he have any doubts?

I know this is the outcome he has wanted. I am glad I have given him that but I'm still not 100 percent with everything. I'm not ready for everything, is still a lot to handle.

Luna Queen. Mating. Pups. A whole Pack. A Mate to care for and care for me.

"Jayden." I break the relaxing silence that had wrapped around us, as if we were in a bubble. I wriggle my body so I lay on my side against him, he moves his head slightly so he is looking into my eyes.

His hand comes back up to stroke another strand of hair away from my face. He hums in reply as he moves his hand to intertwine mine in his.

"I know I've accepted you-" his smile grows impossibly bigger "-but I'm not completely comfortable with the whole Queen Luna thing. I don't think I'm ready for all that yet. Or mating."

I hold my breath as I wait for his reply, but instead of getting upset or angry he grins at me and pecks my lips softly. I enjoy the electric jolt that bursts from his lips.

"I understand completely love." He says caressing my cheek before placing a kiss on the soft kiss "It's a lot to take on, but don't worry about it too much. My mom will teach you everything."

I smile and lift my head up to brush my lips against his, he squeezes my waist and moves us so we are sitting up.

"Can we go for a run?" I ask thinking of the fresh air and the impossible clear sky outside, the storm season has finally decided to take its break from tormenting us.

"Uh love, you've already been on a run." He says raising his eyebrow up at me, I look up and sheepishly smile at him remembering I had run away not even an hour ago.

"I really want to go out plus this time you can come along." I say standing up and making my way to the door. My hand grips the cold doorknob but before I can open it Jayden is in front of me.

"How do I know you won't run again?" He asks, his face pulled into a serious frown one I often see him wear whilst dealing with business in the pack.

"I promise." I say holding up my pinkie finger. Since this morning my mood has skyrocketed dramatically, I feel like singing and dancing around the room. I feel the adrenaline pumping through my veins.

He grins and wraps his larger pinkie around mine. "Fine, but stay with me." He adds giving me a serious look. I nod frantically and leap out the door pulling him along.

It doesn't take us long to get outside even after saying hello to a few pack members. The breeze has turned cold and clouds have once again started to set over the sun.

Damn.

I look at Jayden with sad eyes as I glance back up at the darkening sky. He tilts his head up then turns back to me, "it's fine love. We'll make it a quite run."

"Okay!" I say happily and quickly, without thinking, shift into my wolf ripping all my clothes in the process. Jayden follows suite and barks at me, we both run towards the forest.

Jayden, being an Alpha, is faster but I can tell he is slowing down so I can keep up. I breath deeply trying to push myself harder, running has always been my hobby and I always try to improve.

Suddenly Jayden stops right in front of me, I quickly try to stop but end up ducking so I slide underneath him. He growls and jumps on top of me.

'Stay down.' He mind-links me 'there's a breach at the border a mile ahead. I'm going to check it out. Stay here and don't move.'

'Okay.' I say settling myself on my stomach as he hovers on top of me. 'Go, I'll be fine."

He nods stiffly before racing off and within seconds he is gone, out of sight. I let ours a long sigh as I lay there with my head resting on my paws.

The woods is quiet, quieter than normal. I lift my head and scan the surrounding area. The wind has started to pick up and some leaves fall off a nearby tree.

This part of the woods is deserted, it's just me here as far as I know. Then I hear a twig snap a few metres ahead of my behind a bush.

I stay low and listen again. Another twig snaps, I slowly crawl towards the bush trying to be as silent as possible. I hear a small squeak and ready myself to pounce.

I leap behind the bush to capture whatever was behind it, but to my surprise I only find an immense pain ricochetting up my back leg.

I howl in pain and quickly, on instinct, try to lift my leg up but I can't. It's stuck. I glance back at my back right leg to find it trapped in a bear trap.

The spikes are digging deep into my blood-covered ankle, the scent of blood is hitting me hard and it's becoming a challenge to stay in my wolf form. I know if I shift the pain will worsen as my bones shift.

I cry out in torture as I try to pry the trap of my foot with my front paw, I look at my ankle and stop. I stand, staring at the bloodied broken skin of my ankle as the sharp spikes dig deep into my flesh.

Tears are falling from my eyes but I don't stop them, it hurts too much to concentrate on anything else.

No!

I growl at myself. I'm giving up too easy. I'm not thinking about ways out, I'm only thinking out ways in. I just need to figure out how to escape from the impaled spikes.

Thinking logically. What is the worst that could happen?

1. I could faint from loss of blood and could end up dying.

2. I could rip my ankle out and suffer the consequences, which could include losing my entire ankle.

3. I could try to use my heightened strength to pry the teeth of the trap out of my ankle. But this risks more injuries.

4. (Unlikely) I could stay here and wait for a guard to pass or smell me. Or for Jayden to come back. But the risk is that because I'm so close to the border that a rogue could find me instead.

'Jayden help!' I call out, I know it's a low chance of him getting here soon but I had to have a back up in case I faint from blood loss. I'll try and use my wolf strength to get it off.

'Melody!' Jayden shouts back worriedly but I can't reply. The pain is shooting through my like a million knives.

I quickly grip onto the two sides and let the power in my arms try to pull the teeth away but it was no use. I tried again. And again. And again.

I cry out in frustration and pain as I failed once again to release my foot from the agonisingly painful trap. I can feel my head spin and I'm starting to feel weak.

The effect of this blood loss is kicking in.

'Jay-' I start but don't get to finish because a gigantic black wolf jumps out from the bush in front of me. Jayden. His eyes are black as he stares at me in the eyes, a low pained whine escapes my snout as he steps closer.

I watch as Jayden's eyes slowly move from my eyes down to my trapped back leg. He snarls angrily and almost instantly shifts into his human form. He grabs a pair of trousers from his ankle and throws them on.

He takes the t-shirt off his ankle but throws it near me, I watch carefully as he kneels down next to my back leg. Suddenly a few men show up around us and instantly bow at us.

"Melody, stay still." Jayden commands as he turns to look at me "we're going to get it off you but it's going to hurt."

'Just get it over with.' I say nodding as I lay on the damp ground waiting for sleep. This entire charade has exhausted me, I feel my eyes dropping and my head starts to feel lighter.

Someone grips my shoulders and shakes me awake, I reply with and angry growl. I look up to see a woman holding my head.

"Stay awake Luna, you must stay awake." She says making me huff, obviously the one thing I want I can't get.

I watch as another women comes running over with a first aid bag and she kneels by my ankle. I watch in curiosity as she takes out a needle from the bag.

I snarl and start to stand up, a sharp pain shoots up my leg making me howl in pain. Jayden is quick to come up to my head and push me back down.

"Don't move love. You'll only cause yourself more pain." He says holding my head in his hands "It's just an injection to numb the area."

Soon enough, just as Jayden said, the area around my ankle is completely numb. Although there was still some pain but I didn't want to sound weak.

I lay silently with my head rested on the woman's lap as Jayden and a few other men, guided by whom I think is a nurse, surrounds my ankle.

All of their hands are on the trap as they countdown. This is gonna hurt. The nurse shouts "Now!" And I scream in agony as the teeth eject from my flesh.

I grit my teeth together as the sibs escape my mouth, I feel my whole body weak drastically and seconds later my body is shifting to my human form.

Jayden rushes to my side, throws a t shirt over my naked body and picks me up carefully. Then everything blurs as he runs, he is so fast. I have noticed that he is more powerful.

It scares me but excites me at the same time. I look up with blurry tear-filled eyes at his worried face, this man will be the father of my children.

This man will be my mate. This man will be with me forever. This man will protect me and love me. This man is to be my King and I am to be his Queen.

I start to hear voices then a building comes into sight, the infirmary. I lean my head against Jayden's chest and listen to his fast heart beat.

It's calming. I can feel his muscles through the thin material between his chest and me. I hear his voice shouting orders but the words are jumbled and don't make sense.

Soon he is laying me in a bed, I want to stay in his arms but I'm too tired to keep hold of him. I want to sleep. As soon as his arms have left me doctors and nurses surround me, blocking my view of Jayden.

"Jay." I cough out as my voice suddenly turns dry and hoarse. My eyes are closing as exhaustion finally starts to wrap its arms around me.

He comes into sight just in time before my whole visions turns dark and I fall into unconsciousness.

———————————————

CHAPTER 15

First thing I notice when conscious finds me is that I can't move my legs at all. My eyes are still shut but I'm too scared to open them, what if they had to amputate my leg?!

"Melody." Jayden's soft voice floats into my ear and I instantly feel my muscles relaxing one by one. He is here which means I'm safe.

"Jayden." I cry out then feel his hand grip mine tightly. I squeeze his giant hand and start to cry, the tears couldn't be held in. Not any longer.

"It's okay love. You're okay." Jayden comforts and I feel his warm lips press against my knuckles.

"I want my mom." I cry, allowing the sobs to ricochet through my body. "I want my mom, please Jayden. I want my mom."

I sound like a 5 year old kid who is scared of the dark and is calling her mom to save her. I want my mom right now because I'm scared and because I miss her.

I miss my dad. I miss my brothers. I miss my home.

"Calm down babe, everything will be alright." He whispers comfortingly in my ear as I sob. His arms are securely around my waist now as he comforts me.

A knock on the door breaks me from my thoughts, my eyes instantly snap open and the first thing I see is a blue blanket wrapped tightly around my body.

I can't see my leg but I can tell there must be a cast or something on it by the way the blue blanket bumps up. Thank goodness. One of my arms is wrapped into the blanket while the other lays at my side and my hand being held by Jayden's significantly larger one.

I nod at Jayden as he calls to the person on the other side of the door. I grip his hand tighter as he stands up, I don't want him to leave me. Not now.

The door opens and in comes a middle aged man wearing deep blue scrubs and a white doctors jacket. He also has a stethoscope wrapped around his neck and a clip board in his hand.

"Hello Melody, how are you feeling this morning?" He asks standing at the edge of my bed, I watch as he hangs the clipboard on the rail at the end of my bed.

"I can't move my leg." I say staring at him as he watches me carefully. I can feel Jayden's eyes moving from me to the doctor.

"Yes," he nods "your leg has been bandaged up and strapped down for more efficient healing. you've been asleep for almost half the day so I reckon your pretty much healed by now."

I nod as he explains then he throws the blue blanket off my lower leg revealing the heavy weighted cast. He examines it for a few silent seconds before speaking again.

"Lets open it up shall we!"

20 minutes later I am opened to what lives beneath the white cast and, to my surprise, it's not too bad. My ankle is slightly swelled and bruised, you can see where the teeth of the trap bite into my skin but the wounds have turned into slight cuts.

"How has it healed so fast?" I ask still starring at my ankle and I move my hand to touch it but Jayden grabs it before I can. He growls at me, getting my attention, before shaking his head.

"Well Luna, you were given some of Alphas royal blood. Given that royal alpha blood is stronger than any normal werewolf you healed much faster and the results will be much better." The doctor speaks up and my eyes go straight from the doctor to Jayden.

He smiles down at me and places a kiss on my forehead. His hand stays wrapped around mine as the doctor goes to work with cleaning up the wounds again and then he wrapped some bandage around it. Next he started telling me what to do.

"Right so, you can go home today because I know you'll be taken care of." Doc glances at Jayden "but I must warn for you to be careful, even though you're ankle is healing nicely it is still damaged underneath the skin. Any twist or sudden pressure could cause more injuries. Now I'm not saying bed rest but if you do cause more harm to yourself then that is what will happen."

***

I sigh loudly and fall backwards onto the familiar sheets of Jayden's - our - bed. The silk sheets look around my body as I find a comfy position on top of the covers.

I listen to the soft sound of running water from the shower, as soon as we got in Jayden set me down on the bed, gave me a kiss then disappeared into the adjoining bathroom.

I feel my body cry in exhaustion as I move to crawl out of bed. I drag myself into the closet and the smell of pure manliness hits me.

I run my hand along the neatly folded tops on his shelves and the hoodies that hang up on the silver rails.

Even though Jayden did originally take me to my room as soon as I had got changed into some pyjamas Jayden decided it would be better if I stayed in his room.

It's not like I don't sleep in his room every night anyway. When I'm alone I get nightmares.

I bite my lip and glance at the door to check if Jayden is coming. I quickly strip out of my clothes into one of Jayden's soft grey tops.

I turn towards the door to head out back into the bedroom. I still and my face heats up instantly, there in front of me is Jayden.

He is smirking at me from the doorway wearing only a towel around his waist. I blush deeper and divert my eyes, by habit I start to bite my lip.

"Stealing my top are you?" He chuckles walking over to me then as soon as I'm in reach his arms snake around my waist.

"Maybe." I say trying not to stutter because of the sparks racing through my body at his naked touch.

"Hmm." He says dipping his head into my neck, his hand finds the bottom of the shirt and he tugs it slightly "I like you in my clothes."

I laugh and wrap my arms around his neck "well I better wear them more often hadn't I? Or maybe I'll go back to my room and change." I say trying to move away.

He growls and his grip tightens around me as he leans back to look at me.

"No, you are in our room love. Plus there is no need to change." He says kissing my lips quickly before pulling away.

"Well do you know who does need to change? You! Get a move on! You've got me all wet now!" I say pushing him away softly.

He laughs and pulls on the shirt again, he quickly leans over me and grabs another one. He throws it over my face then I hear his heart warming laugh.

I pout as I remove the top from my head, which dishevels my hair making it fall in my face.

He chuckles and uses his finger to remove the hair from my face then he cups my cheeks. His head dips down and he softly bites my pouted lip.

I throw my arms around his waist and pull him closer to kiss him. He instantly kisses back and I hear him groan gently.

The kiss is passionate with some hints of dominance from Jayden, his Alpha power always surprises me even though his scent gives off raw power.

I pull away needing to catch my breath, we stand in each other's embrace for a few more minutes before I finally break the silence.

"We need to get changed." I say breathlessly glancing at the forgotten top on the floor. Thank goodness Jayden's towel is still securely around his waist.

"Okay." He says pecking my lips once more before turning around and starts rummaging through his clothes. I quickly leave completely forgetting the top on the floor and keeping the thick grey one I am wearing on.

I quickly make my way to the bed and fall down on top of it, the soft fluffiness yearns for me to get in and my body wants to sleep.

I crawl under the covers and snuggle into the pillow, sleep slowly starts washing over me until the bed dips beside me.

I open my eyes slightly and peck at Jayden who give me a smile as he gets under the covers. He lays down and puts his arms around my waist then pulls me closer.

"My parents want to talk to us tomorrow." He says kissing my forehead. I let out a long sigh.

"Okay but for now, can we sleep?" I say laying my head on his unnaturally strong chest.

"Of course love, get some rest." He says.

***

I groan silently as my bladder groans in protest of my sleep. I roll over onto my stomach but it just adds pressure to my bladder.

I finally decide to give in. I open my eyes and have to wait for them to adjust to the darkness of the night. Good thing I have wolf vision.

I glance up at Jayden's sleeping face, his mouth is slightly open and his features are so relaxed.

I remove myself from his arms and make my way to the bathroom. I quickly complete my business and wash my hands.

Suddenly I let out a pained scream and fall to the floor. The pain is unbearable. Tears have instantly started falling down my cheeks as I sob in the darkness.

Need Jayden.

I scream again as the pain worsens in my lower abdomen. I curse under my breath just as the lights in the bathroom flicker on.

"Shit, Melody!" Jayden's voice fills the bathroom and soon I feel his touch on my hot skin. It instantly starts relieving the pain.

Then it hits me, I'm in heat. That's why I want Jayden.

"Melody -shit- you're burning up." He says picking me up, he runs to the bed and throws me down. When I look at him his eyes are black and filled with lust.

"Heat." I mumble just as another scream rips from my throat. He grips my hand and suddenly he is hovering over me.

"Shhh baby, it's okay you're going to be okay." He says then his hands find the front of my top and he rips it off.

"N-no pls." I say, I don't want us to mate like this. Not because we have to or because it would stop my heat.

I can do this. I survived those years thinking I didn't have a mate, I can survive a few night of agony.

"I would never force you." He says breathlessly, I can tell this is hard for him too. I lift my head up and bring my lips to his, instantly the pain dies down slightly.

He kisses me back deeply and rather rough, I can feel part of his wolf in the kiss. His tongue dives into my mouth and wins the dominance battle.

His hands are gripping my waist tightly as he holds himself above me, he lowers slightly and I feel his naked chest against my own bare stomach.

I realise that I am only in my bra and knickers and he is only wearing a pair of joggers. I pull away trying to regain the oxygen in my lungs.

Jayden climbs off me and lays on his side against my side. I don't move from my position on my back, scared that movement will bring back the agony.

One of Jayden's arms moves to pillow my head and one of his hands rubs my abdomen in a gentle caress.

"You'll be okay Melody."

CHAPTER 16

R ain batters against the window opposite the bed. It wakes me up from my light slumber, I groan in pain as I stretch myself out.

I can still feel the heat in the pit of my stomach but so far it's died down. It's no where near as painful as it was last night.

When I was 16 I did get the period and Heat talk with my parents. Which was the most awkward few hours of my life! They also decided to add some mating advice to it too.

Mikey, of course, just laughed and smirked the entire time, I on the their hand sat still blushing crimson red.

I snuggle closer into the pillow trying to let sleep find me again but an arm around my waist had another idea.

Jayden's arm pulls me over so I'm lying on my back, I pout up at him but to my dismay he just smiles. Slowly he leans down and places a gentle kiss on the side of my lips.

Then he moves to kiss my lips but this time the kiss is passionate and deep instead of gentle. I wrap my arms around his neck and pull him impossibly closer.

He manoeuvers his body so he hovers above me, my legs find themselves wrapping around his waist and pulling him tighter against me.

I could feel his lust just as he can probably sense mine. We need to stop soon or I don't think we will be able too.

"Stop." I whisper against his lips moving my hand onto his chest. He pulls away slowly as if he didn't want too, I knew he didn't but I wasn't ready yet.

"Good morning." He says with a soft smile and he lays on his side next to me. His hand is softly caressing my lower abdomen and the other hand props his head up.

"Morning Jay." I say starring at his solid chest, I place my hand on it and feel his fast heart beat beneath my hand.

"We were meant to speak to my parents his morning but I've postponed it to this afternoon instead." Jayden says looking at the clock on the wall. "They said about 12 and that they are having a picnic sort of, so we'll meet them in the indoor gardens."

"Okay sound fine, but will they...uh smell me?" I say and I can feel myself blushing as soon as the words leave my mouth.

He chuckles and places a kiss on my forehead before fully sitting up and pulling me with him.

"Maybe but don't worry, my parents know what it's like so they won't judge you." He says comfortingly.

I nod and turn away. Suddenly I realise that I haven't talked to my brother since he started being Alpha. I grab my phone and start typing a text message.

"What you doing?" Jay asks kissing my shoulder then my neck, he turns me around to face him and smiles down at me.

"Just texting Mikey, he became Alpha the day after we left and I haven't spoken to him since considering..."

"Considering what?" He asks places yet another kiss on my neck, he seriously can't keep himself off me this morning. It must be the heat.

"Considering everything that is happening here, I'm always busy." I say just as a buzz echoes from my phone.

I quickly look at my phone to see a message from Mikey.

"Oh my gosh." I whisper looking at the message and re-reading, twice. I can't believe it! I've been gone 10 days and they are already engaged!

Mikey didn't even tell me, we use to tell each other everything. But I suppose circumstances change.

Victoria wants me at her hen party, oh my gosh, that would be wicked fun! Only one problem, I don't think Jayden is going to let me go home and out of his sight any time soon.

"What is it?" Jay asks from the closet doorway, I hadn't even noticed that he had gotten out of bed. I look at him then back to the phone.

"I have to go home." It slips out, those 5 little words. Only 1 short sentence but the snarl that echoes around the room after them is not as short lived.

"What?!" He says threateningly, his hands are gripping onto the door frame so tightly that it's starting to crack beneath the force.

"Calm down." I say forcing my voice not to break or stutter as my heart races at the sight of how utterly terrifying he looks.

His wolf has partly come out, his claws are sharp and digging into the wall. His fangs have slipped out of his mouth. His eyes are growing darker.

I should of waited until after my heat was over, I forgot about it to be honest. I was told that males become unbearably possessive when their female is in heat. They would literally kill if any other male tried to take the female away from him.

That's exactly what I just tried to do. From his perspective I'm guessing it sounded like I said that I would leave him and go home.

"Calm down! Melody I have told you this before and I will tell you again, you are mine. You will stay with me because if you leave I will kill to get you back. Our souls are connected. I'm not forcing you into anything you don't want to do because I care about you, more than I expected for our first week together." He says standing in front of me all of a sudden "I'm sorry if you think I'm over reacting Melody but you are in heat and still unmated and it's driving my wolf crazy."

He sighs loudly and rests his head in my lap, I run my hand through his hair softly and place a kiss on his head.

"Jay," I say caressing his almost hidden cheek "I meant I have to go home soon to visit my brother. He texted me saying he is getting married. I'm invited to the hen party, I'm sure you can come along but not to the hen obviously."

I laugh softly as he slowly lifts his head to meet my eyes. I place my fingers under his chin and lean forward to capture his lips in my own.

I don't know what's happened to make me so...loving? Is that the right word? After accepting him and coming into heat everything is just starting to finally settle.

I do have a mate.

Jayden is my mate.

I pull my lips away before we start anything because I have a brother to text and a picnic to prepare for.

"I'm sorry, I'm just scared okay?" Jayden says getting up as I do and following me into the closet "I've never been this out of control, you literally drive me crazy."

He chuckles and throws me a cheeky smirk "but I know we'll make it through this following both our wishes, well more yours because mine would include you na-"

"Jayden!" I say throwing a sock at him, he lets out a laugh and puts his hands up in mock surrender. "Right, out! I'm getting changed."

"Okay okay! I'll be out here if you need me." He shouts once he is out of sight.

I grab a pair of ripped black skinny jeans and throw on one of Jay's oversized top that falls off my shoulder. I finish the outfit with some simple black converse.

My waves of hair are naturally flowing over my shoulder so I decide to leave it how it is. I grab my phone from where I threw it before changing and text Mikey back.

After hitting send I glance in the mirror to my left and check out my outfit, it looks normal and casual.

Do I look alright? I'm about to eat with the Alpha King and Queen that also happen to be my mates parents.

I let out a laugh while shaking my head and text a quick reply.

I push my phone into my back pocket. I walk out of the closet and instantly notice Jayden playing a game on his phone while laying on the bed.

"Ready?" I ask standing at the end of the bed, I bend down and lean my arms against his knees that fall off the bed.

"Ready for what?" He asks propping himself up on his elbows.

"To meet your parents obviously!" I say.

"Melody," he laughs "that's in like over 3 hours! You complete dumbo! I told you we're going to chill because you're still in heat."

I groan and fall on top of him. He lets out a pained huff but he quickly shifts me so I'm lying comfortably on top of him.

"When will the pain come back?" I ask fiddling with his white shirt before falling off him to lie by his side.

"It will come and go. In the nights it will be at its worst but don't worry it's only 2 more nights." He says comfortingly, rubbing my back but it doesn't quite rid my fear.

As a kid I was told that the pain of heat can eventually lead to a female dying from the excruciatingly painful experience.

"Okay, you won't leave me will you?" I ask in a whisper as I look up at his deep blue eyes that blaze down on me.

"I promise I will never leave you." He says "Unless it's to punch someone who is looking at you for too long."

"Jay!" I groan with a laugh and hid my face in his chest. I feel his chest rumble as he laughs with me and his heart is beating powerful and steadily.

"Who is coming to the picnic?" I ask. Before he answers I sneak a glance outside to the still pouring rain.

"Well it will be my Beta Asher and his mate of three years Willow, they are expecting their first baby but she is only about 9 weeks along." Jayden says looking up at the ceiling "Then it's my parents and us, my Delta Mason and Gamma Blaine won't be able to join us today considering your in heat and they are unmated."

"Oh okay that's fine." I say with a nod.

"My mom gave me some spray that masks your scent which she said could help decrease your heat scent." He says getting up, he goes into the bathroom and comes out with a perfume bottle in his hand.

He chucks it to me and I catch it with ease. I get off the bed and spray the bottle's liquid all over me to cover my scent.

"How is it?" I say as I finish, I put my arms out and spin around for show. He takes a sniff and scrunched us his nose.

"I can smell it but that's because I'm your mate. It's definitely died down though, for now anyways." He replies.

"Okay good." I nod then glance over at him to notice that he is staring at me with a small smile on his face.

I turn to fully face him and tilt my head to the side, he just grins at me even more and folds his arms over his chest.

"You drive me crazy." He says with a slight shake of his head. "You don't realise how badly I want us to fully mate, to start our life together."

"Me too but I just need more time." I say walking to him and slipping my arms around his waist.

"I know and I'll wait forever, every full moon. Werewolf joke there." He chuckles "My little moonlight."

"What did you just call me?" I say raising an eyebrow up at him.

"My little moonlight."

"Stop acting like such a lycan! You're a werewolf you dumbo!" I laugh.

"Sorry sorry." He says filling his head into my neck and breathing deeply, I sigh in content in his comforting arms.

"Kiss me." I command looking up, he immediately lifts his head up and smirks like a child at Christmas.

He leans down and presses his lips to mine.

CHAPTER 17

The clouds have risen once more and the sky has decided to play hide and seek. The clouds open up and allow the rain to fall down on Jayden and I.

We were having a nice walk to his parents indoor gardens but the rain decided it wanted us to hurry up.

I pull the thin coat over my head as my attempt to keep my hair from getting dry. But the rain will always find its way in.

The garden doors are finally in reach and Jayden and I burst into them as quickly as we can. We both let out a few deep breathes of relief at the instant warmth of which the gardens behold.

I look around at the greenery of the gardens and smile. Flowers of all sorts are splattered around, living amongst bushes and trees.

I finally realise that the King, Queen, Jay's Beta and his pregnant mate are sitting on a picnic bench in the middle of the gardens.

"Hey!" Jayden waves over at his smiling parents, he takes my hand and walks us both over to where his parents are sitting.

My stomach is fluttering with nerves as I watch his parents standing up to greet us. My eyes glance over at the Beta Asher whom is smiling at Jayden and I with his arm tightly wrapped around a beautiful woman. I guess that is Willow.

"Mom!" Jay greets hugging the short thin woman that looks exactly like him; he takes after his mom then. I watch as he turns around and gives his father a man hug.

Then he turns to me and wraps his arm around my waist, he shuffles me forward slightly and I smile at his parents. Even though I've met them briefly before it is still nerve-racking.

"Hey!" I greet just before I'm pulled in for a hug by Kate, I instantly return the warm hug and enjoy the familiar feeling of a mom hug.

I miss my mom.

"How are you Melody?" King Russell asks as I pull away from Kate's hug.

"I'm.."

What am I? Am I happy? I glance at Jayden who is grinning down at me. I'm happy when I'm with Jayden but I feel like something is missing. Family, more importantly my family.

"...fine" I reply with a smile as I push away the negative thoughts cramming my head.

"Come sit down; you must be starving." Kate says putting a shoulder around me and leading me over to the picnic table where Asher and Willow have stayed seated.

"Hey Melody, nice to finally meet you." Asher speaks up finally, he stands up and walks over to give me a hug. As he hugs me I hear the slight quiet growl escape Jayden's mouth making me giggle.

"Yes it's good to meet you!" I reply glancing from him to Jayden who has sat down opposite Willow.

"I know its been a long time coming but you've been busy with training and Jayden then I've been off duties since you got back to help sort out Willow. The baby was a surprise, one we are glad for but it's also one we weren't ready for." Asher says leading me to the picnic table where everyone is already seated.

I leave Asher and take a seat next to Jayden, he greets me with a quick kiss on the forehead before proceeding to chat with Asher. I look over at Willow and notice she is smiling at me.

"Hey Melody, I'm Willow!" She speaks up with the same happy smile as she leans over and shakes my hand. "It's nice to see you at last, Jayden's done a good job at keeping you to himself as much as possible hasn't he?"

I let out a laugh and turn to a now pouting Jayden, I lean up and peck his cheek before turning back to Willow.

"I know! It's good to finally meet my fellow Beta female, we should definitely go out sometime without the boys. I promise there will be no alcohol." I laugh gesturing towards her small bump.

"Sounds great! No alcohol but plenty of boys!" Just as she finishes her sentence Jayden and Asher growl possessively.

"So Melody," Kate speaks up just as I grab a sandwich from the middle and place it on my plate "how is your heat?"

"Mom!" Jayden yells in embarrassment but Kate only laughs at her son.

"What? It is an innocent question everyone at this table has either been through it or witnessed it." She speaks truthfully but I can't help the blush that creeps up my neck as all gazes fall on me to answer the question.

"Um...its manageable." I nod biting into my sandwich. Asher, Russell and Willow all nod and carry on eating but Kate didn't seem to want to drop the subject so easily.

"I don't like you putting you and Jayden in such pain just because you don't want to fully mate yet." She says shaking her head in disappointment "It is pointless because in the end you will both mate anyways so why wait and sit in pain."

I look down at my food as her words swirl around in my head, am I being stupid? Why am I postponing the inevitable? She is right; we will mate one day so why am I letting me and also Jayden go through all this pain because I want to wait?

"You can't say that Kate!" Russell scolds his wife "It's their bond so it's Jayden and Melody's choice."

"Yes I know that!" Kate shouts giving me an annoyed look before turning back to Russell "But it is not both of their choice is it?! Jayden obviously wants to mat with her; he doesn't want her to wait and continue with the pain of heat! But no, it's just her choice. She is choosing pain over love!"

My heart is thumping out of my chest now and my ears have tuned out of the constant shouting. Kate's words fly through my head at top speed and I can feel a panic attack creeping its way into my chest.

I don't really notice when I had stood up but I find myself racing out of the glass doors and into the pouring rain. It felt numbing on my face.

I could hear a faint voice calling out to me but my feet were working on autopilot. Kate's voice in my head has turned to words and its screaming now, screaming about how horrible and stupid I am.

I breathe deeply and find myself realising that I am in the woods, the rain is still pouring and it's starting to bite at my skin now but my head is too occupied to think about getting warm.

I lean against the tree and try to clear my thoughts to focus on my breathing. It starts getting slower and finally my chest stops squeezing allowing me to once again breathe normally.

My head still pounds with the negative thoughts and the way my mates mom was shouting at me and about me.

I open my eyes for the first time in 10 minutes and look around to try and figure out where I am. There are trees all around me, I wish I knew what part of the forest I am in.

Well I was in the gardens which are situated in the northern area of the castle grounds; I must be in the northern or east forest then.

It's dark underneath the thick layer of black rain cloud; it reminds me of when I was little when I was scared of the dark.

I use to cry and cry until Mikey crawled from his bed on the opposite side of the room into mine and cuddled me.

Eventually when I was 16 I became too scared to sleep because of the nightmares that haunted me every night. I went days at a time with no sleep until eventually my parents took me to the infirmary.

The doctor injected me with some sort of sedative and I slept for 2 days on and off in the infirmary. My parents suspected that my dreams were linked to the mystic wolf.

But it wasn't. I was just suffering of severe depression because I had declared I had no mate. It's weird something in me thought that meant my mate is dead so I feel into a depressed state.

After a 2 years I finally got a hold of myself and the nightmares faded into blackness. Then Jayden walked into my life and they started again but this time they were different.

They were about me because isolated for not having a mate. Now they are about losing my mate who I am suddenly falling for.

A cold shiver scraps up my back as the cold rain finally sleeps through my clothes and touches my bare skin underneath.

I let myself slide down the tree until I am sitting on the soaked glacial forest floor, it doesn't make a difference though; I'm soaking wet anyways.

How am I going to face anyone now? I'm being such a selfish bitch. I didn't think about the pain my heat is causing Jayden or the entire pack for that matter. If I die then Jayden dies and the Royal line and pack is left with no heir.

I bite down on my lip, hard to try and focus on my pain instead of the thoughts in my mind. My wolf isn't helping, she is anxious and upset so she has disappeared into the back of my mind.

"S***!" I hear a familiar voice swearing, the person was a black blur in the distance but their voice was as clear as day.

One minute the shadow is in the distance then the next thing I know is that they are directly in front of me. It's Jayden.

"Melody! Oh my gosh Melody. It's okay love." He says hurriedly. He picks me up gently as though I'm a china doll about to break.

I feel my eyes starting to roll back but I force myself to stay awake, its peaceful. My ears are no longer allowing any noise in so I just watch and feel the cold rain biting at my skin.

Jayden is pelting at full speed so all I can see is a green blur of the forest until finally he stops; we are outside the infirmary.

People have stopped and started starring now. Everyone is holding umbrellas and its amazing; there are so many colours everywhere.

I rest my tired head on Jayden's chest as he runs in the infirmary doors. In an instant we are greeted by nurses who hurriedly lay me on a trolley.

I only watch in silent as they cover me in blankets and foil sheets then I'm wheeled down some corridors. My whole body feels numb but I can feel the constant shivers ricochetting through my body.

I cough violently as my chest starts compressing my lungs. I can feel the rain dripping off the end of my nose and falling to its doom on the thin mattress of the trolley.

I come to a sudden stop and I feel nothing as the doctor and nurses shuffle me onto a hospital bed. The doctor is talking but I can't hear him, I've tuned out by now.

He starts cutting up my clothes and Jayden growls angrily. In seconds he has me changed into the t-shirt he was wearing 10 seconds ago. The doctors then put blankets over all my body and my head.

"Right," The doctor starts as he examines me over "her body temperature is at 28ºC. Her breathing is too shallow, can you put an oxygen mask on her please."

Before I know it a mask is put over my head and covers my nose and mouth. I try and take deep breaths but find it difficult.

"Alpha Jayden." I listen to a women in light blue scrubs talking to my mate "Luna has got moderate hypothermia. She will be fine but for a few days she will be constantly tired and feel cold. Also we aren't sure but her heat might not come as she is too cold."

"Okay great thank you." He replies with a nod, he walks over to me and takes a seat next to me.

"We'll pull through this Melody, don't listen to my mother. This is us, you and me, not her. "

CHAPTER 18

Consciousness finds me the next morning in Jayden's bed unlike when I fell asleep in.

The first thing I notice is Jayden fast asleep on the chair next to me with his head on the edge of my bed; I look around the room and smile at the sunshine outside.

I lean over and place a kiss on Jayden's head; he instantly wakes up. He looks at me with a sleep grin before letting out a loud yawn and a stretch.

"Morning princess." He says kissing my cheek then moves to kiss my lips. I smile into the kiss and wrap my arms around his neck.

"Morning." I reply with a grin after pulling away from his luscious lips.

"So baby," He says climbing into the bed next to me. "how are you feeling?"

"I'm alright, just feel a bit off I guess." I reply looking down to where I lay.

"Are you sure? Don't pretend to be alright for me, tell me the truth."

"I promise I am fine Jay and I promise that I will tell you if I don't feel alright." I say cupping his cheek in my hand.

"We were suppose to tell you at the picnic then all this happened but tonight you're parents and brothers are coming to the castle for the night!"

"No way!" I scream standing up way to quickly, my head instantly spins and I grip the edge of the bed to steady myself.

"Woah!" Jayden says grabbing me "Doc says that you will get tired and dizzy spells."

"I'm okay." I nod letting a smile find my face "So what shall we do today?"

"Well we could go out if you like." He suggests "Even though you should stay in but if I'm honest I think we need to get out of the castle. My mom is trying to find you by the way, to apologise."

I rub my temples at the thought about Kate and what happened yesterday, I don't think I want to talk to her yet.

What could we do?

"I heard Willow talking about something that's happening today." I say folding my arms in front of me.

Jayden raises his eyebrows and looks at my chest, I snap my fingers in front of him which makes him look back at my face. I roll my eyes but can't help the smile that finds my face.

"Yes there is a big sort of party thing; we do it every few months. Basically all the guys play a big basketball match while the females sit on the side having picnics and stuff." He explains with a shrug "I haven't been for a while actually."

"Lets go then!" I say jumping up but stop when Jayden gives me a stern look.

"You realise this will be the day you will be introduced to the entire pack then don't you?" Jay says gripping my waist slightly tighter.

I never thought about that but I suppose that wouldn't be such a bad thing. It's not an entire day all about me so the main focus won't be on me.

It sounds like a good idea.

"That's fine by me." I smirk and place a kiss on his chin.

The biggest brightest smile lights up his face as soon as I say that. He leans down and pecks my lips softly before heading into the closet.

I sigh and rub my hand down my face. I can't believe this is actually happening? I'm going to have to face Kate and the truth behind her words, I just hope the whole pack aren't on the same page as her.

I shake my head to rid myself of those thoughts and walk straight into the bathroom. I really need a long hot shower.

***

"Lodi you okay?" Jay asks wrapping his arms around my waist from behind me. I smile and lean back against his solid chest.

I look out of the window and hold onto the frame, I cherish the feeling of fresh air and Jayden's arms around me.

"I'm fine." I say with a short nod. Jayden moves his arms to my waist and spins me around so I am facing him.

"Shall we get going?" He smirks holding his hands out in front of me to take. I smile and put my hands in his large ones, I can't help but love the way his fit worth mine.

Cheesy right?

Jayden leads me down the many flights of stairs before taking me outside. The sun beams down on us making me regret wearing a thick knitted jumper.

The sky is a gorgeous blue which is a change from the constant grey clouds we've had this winter.

"It's lovely today." I say as Jay and I walk towards the basketball court holding hands.

"It is indeed, the perfect day for a game and a picnic. Just a warning everyone is going to be here including my parents." He says looking down at me.

"How many people?"

"We're the royal pack so we are the largest around with just over 10,000 inhabitants around. But most live in other territories for schools and uni." He explains and I gasp.

10,000 wolves!? He expects me to lead 10,000 wolves! That's not even mentioning other packs we have to help with.

"Holy crackers." I whisper to myself, I know Jay heard but I didn't mean for him too.

"Hey." He says stopping us and moving to stand in front of me "It's okay Lodi, I promise to never leave your side. We will rule he best we can and that's all we can do."

I smile and peck his cheek. He nods in approval before carrying on walking. His words play no part in calming my nerves though.

After a while of walking, I hear the party before I see it. People are talking everywhere and I can hear the shouts of the guys on the court.

"Hey!" Willow pops up out of nowhere and pulls me into a hug. She turns to give Jay a quick hug too.

"Hello." I reply with a smile "How's thepicnic looking?"

"Great but I could really use an extra pair of hands on the buffet table." She says, her tone full of the unspoken question of help.

"Sure I'll help." I say making her shout in happiness. I look to find Jayden to see him talking to another male in a pair of basketball shorts.

"Thank you! Everyone has left me to do it to watch the boys." She says obviously annoyed.

"Hey Jay," I call to my distracted mate. He turns and gives me a smile "I'm going to help Willow with the food."

Jay frowns and walks to me so he stands directly in front of me. His hands fins the side of my face in a gentle hold.

"You sure you'll be okay? You realise my mom is here." He questions, his thumb runs along my cheek softly and I sigh mentally.

"I'll be fine, anyway you're only on rn court so I know where to find you." I reply with a slight shrug. "Go have fun with the other guys."

"Okay," he smiles and pecks my lips "but come find me if there are any problems alright?"

"Alright." I nod. I give him a quick hug before turning and walking away with Willow. I can't help but glance behind me and watch as he disappears into the crowd around the court.

"Are you usually on food duty then?" I ask Willow as we walk towards a series of tables in a line, covered in all sorts of food.

"Yeah, party food is my speciality. I love to make little snacks and finger foods but I hate making actual meals." She finished saying just as we arrive at the tables of food.

"What do you want me to do?" I ask with a smile.

"Could you put all of the drinks from in the bag under there into the jugs please. Then put all the red cups on the table too." She points to my right then continues to move food around.

I grab some jugs off the table and line them up in a line before getting all the large bottles of fizzy drinks out of the bag.

As I start filling up the jugs I hear shouting and cheering from the crowds. I look in the direction of the court and make out the men all jumping to shoot a hoop.

"Hello." I hear a voice behind me making me jump. I turn around to see a little girl with pigtails standing behind me. "Please may I have some orange juwce?"

"Of course you can!" I say happily, quickly filling up a little cup before handing it to the little girl "Don't spill it will you."

"No I prwmise I won't." She says with a toothy grin just before she rushes off towards a gathering crowd of women on picnic blankets.

I stare at the crowd for a few seconds but instead of heading over there I return to pouring out the drinks.

"Hey." Jayden's warm voice floats around me and his arms find my waist. He rests his chin on my shoulder and I turn my head to kiss his nose.

His face is slightly sweaty and I notice that he is shirtless. I frown; I don't want all these women staring at my mates body.

Only I can see my mates body. I want to see it, all of it.

I feel something rush down my spine and thought flood my mind of us mating. I want us to mate, I do want us to mate event though I'm still scared.

There is no point being scared. I know that this man in front of me will always be there for me and will always love me.

"I missed you." Jay says. His warm embrace making me sigh in content. Kisses my shoulder softly as we sway slightly in the soft breeze.

I turn around and wrap my arms around his neck. His bright eyes stare down at me lovingly making my heart burst.

I go on my tiptoes and place my lips on his. He immediately kisses back; at first it was slowly but it soon turned into a battle of dominance.

He wins, obviously. His arms tighten around my waist and back then he pulls my flush into him. My hands move to his cheeks as we kiss.

As we kiss I forget about everything. About Kate. About the basketball game. About the drinks.

Everything except how I want this man, forever.

I pull away slowly, not really wanting too but needing the oxygen. Jay rests his head against my own and breathes deeply.

"Jay." I whisper, biting my lip nervously. He hums his response as he keeps his forehead on mine. "I'm ready." I whisper softly.

Instantly his ferocious blue eyes snap to mine and I feel his grip tighten against my waist.

"What?" He says in a surprised whisper. His eyes are searching mine but they won't find anything but honesty in them.

"I don't want to wait anymore Jay, I have you and I want you before I lose you." I say reaching up and placing a quick kiss on his lips.

"I promise you'll never lose me. Are you sure you're ready?"

"Yes." I say and he smiles so brightly that the sun is probably getting jealous.

"Let's not do it on the picnic food though." He laughs and his humour tickles my stomach so I let out my own laugh.

"Shut up Jay or I'll change my mind." I hit his shoulder playfully. He gasps then smirks, he leans back and bows his head to me.

"Whatever you say my Queen."

"You're such a goofball." I giggle wrapping my arms around his neck tightly again.

"I'm your goofball. Soon I'll be your goofball forever!" He says picking me up by my waist and spinning me around.

I squeal happily and when he stops I tilt my head down and press my lips gently against his.

CHAPTER 19

"Jayden! Melody!" A feminine voices pulls us from our make out session, I frown at the woman now standing a few feet in front of us.

Jay growls through our mind-link and puts me on the ground. Although he keeps his arms around my waist as he move to stand beside me.

'If you're too uncomfortable with this tell me, okay?.' Jay links me and I just answer him wth a quick nod of my head.

"Mom." Jayden greets her with a sort of sad smile on his face. That facial expression changed my mind on Kate, she's been horrible to me but I'll put it behind me for Jay's happiness.

"Jayden I wish to apologise to you for how I acted the other day." She says avoiding my eye.

"Thank you mom." He replies with a nod then I notice him gesture to me with his head. I stare straight at Kate who turns to me with a smile.

"Melody. I apologise for saying what I did to you." She says giving me a slight nod "I shouldn't have interfered."

"Thank you." I reply with the best smile I could master. I have to forgive her, after all she is the queen and my mom-in-law.

"Melody! Over here!" I hear Willows smooth voice calling me from the court field. I nod in respect to Kate and walk straight over to Willow without looking at Jayden.

I don't hear any footsteps behind me; I can't help but feel slightly annoyed at that. I shake my head and walk to Willow who is by the tables of food.

"Hey, you okay?" I ask as I reach her. She sighs loudly and shakes her head.

"No! Someone has eaten all the bloody chips already! Would you go to the kitchens and get some more please?" She asks rushing around trying to move plates and stuff.

I grab her by the shoulders making her stop. "Willow, just breath for a minute." I order her with a smile. "You're pregnant for god sake, you shouldn't be doing this so go watch the game with the others and I'll sort this out. Okay?"

"Okay." She breathes out in relief the she gives me a quick hug. "Thanks Melody, you're gonna be an amazing Queen."

I watch her waddle off to the cheering crowd around the basketball games. I smile as I watch her but I catch the glimpse of my mates sexy self on the courts enjoying himself.

I sigh before making my way to the castle kitchens. I get there pretty quickly because my mind is half asleep.

I head straight to the chips cupboard and grab a few bags of assorted flavours. I place them on the kitchen island and lean my head on the cold surface.

Out of nowhere I hear a knock on the long wall of floor-to-ceiling windows. I spin around quickly and take a few steps to the windows; I look around but see nothing.

Suddenly a couple of large rock hurtles into the window smashing each one of the giant windows. The rock smashes into my shoulder so hard that I collapse onto the floor of smashed glass.

My head was pounding and my ears started to buzz. I felt like everything around me was in slow motion and I couldn't breathe for a minute.

Nobody is around so it's just me here. That means no other casualties, thank goodness.

I lay in the floor and breathe slowly as I look around. The windows have smashed and the glass is everywhere. I feel the sting of the cuts from the glass over my body.

I feel the warm blood dripping from my face onto the floor. My shoulder is burning and tears have formed in my eyes from the pain. I steadily move my arms from over my head as place them on the floor.

I ignore the glass cutting through my hands and knees as I stand up. My head is spinning and I feel my whole body sting as I start to walk.

Blood is trickling down my arms, head and my legs. My thick jumper is torn and so are my leggings but my black combat boots are protecting my feet.

I get outside and the cheering of the crowds hits my ears. I sigh in relief of the help I can get from there. But then I stop.

The pain isn't that bad and the only thing that is bad is the amount of blood on me, it makes me look like I was just murdered.

I look over the field at the crowds around the court and the many people at the picnic blankets on the ground. I don't want to cause any hassle.

I look to my right and see the infirmary in the near distance. I nod at the thought of going there and slowly make my way towards the large building.

'Baby, where have you gone?' Jayden asks through our mind-link, I look at the infirmary and carry on walking as I reply. My foot is hurting so I try not to since through the link.

'I won't be long.' I reply as I get closer to the infirmary steps, I quickly block my feeling and emotions from the mind link again.

I take my time walking in to the infirmary but as soon as I enter gasps erupt everywhere. Immediately nurses are rushing up to me.

"Stop." I say loudly so everyone can hear me "No need to cause alarm okay? I am fine just got cut by glass."

They all sigh in relief and one starts to lead me down the corridor then into a room. I realise at that moment that I didn't tell anyone about the smashed windows.

"Hey," I say to the nurse as she sits me on the bed "could you send someone to the castle kitchens? The glass windows smashed. Oh! Don't tell them I told you!"

"Of course, Luna. Now lay back and the doctor will be right in." I nod and watch as she exits the room with a rather confused expression.

'Melody. This isn't funny, where are you?! Willow and I are worried.' Jayden shouts through our mind link making me jump. I fall backwards onto the hard bed.

'I'm fine Jay, I'll be back to the courts in a bit.' I say, sighing.

'But where are you now? Please tell me baby.'

Just as I am about to reply the doctor comes into the room with a smile. I quickly sober up and send an awkward wave to the doctor.

"Hello Luna, I'm Doctor Lillian. What have you done to yourself?" She asks walking over to me. She looks over my arms and face first.

"Could you remove your jumper and leggings if that's possible, Luna." She says and I nod "Some of these are sill healing but most of them are healed already."

I quickly change and lay back down on the bed. Doctor Lillian examines me quietly and cautiously. I wince when she touches my shoulder and she apologised many times. Annoying but I'll let her off as she is healing me.

I hear Jayden in my mind but I don't answer him, yet.

"Right there is a piece of glass in your ankle so just keep still, I am going to numb the area with an injection then remove it. I will then stitch it up." She explains.

Minutes later she has finished stitching up the wound on my foot. She places the used utensils back into the silver tray on the side.

"That's you all patched up Luna, you are free to leave but try not to open your stitches by over doing exercise for a few days. Oh and your shoulder is severely bruised so that will take longer than normal to heal." She says giving me a smile. "Now, there are spare clothes over there and if you don't mind me saying, you best go find Alpha Jayden."

"Thank you very much. Oh and call me Melody." I say hopping off the bed. She waves goodbye quickly before exiting the room.

'I'm on my way back now.' I link Jayden and suddenly anger and worry rushed through the link from his side.

'Melody?! Stay where you are! I'm coming to get you, just tell me where you are. There has been an attack.' He is almost screaming now.

'Yeah about that...' I say hurrying to change and I practically sprint to the castle courts. Using werewolf speed, it only takes me a minute even though my ankle starts burning now.

I look around at the people still enjoying the game but I see Asher standing at he steps of the castle, scanning the crowd.

His eyes land on me and I see him shout something. Immediately after Jayden storms out of the doors of the castle and runs straight towards me.

As soon as I am arms width away he picks me up bridal style and races back into the castle. Before I can acknowledge anything I land on Jayden's bed.

I giggle slightly but stop as soon as I notice Jayden's expression. It's a mixture between angry and worry which makes him look slightly odd.

"Melody, where the heck have you been for the past 2 hours?" He asks quite calmly as he leans down so he level with me. His arms are either side of me and he keeps getting closer.

"That's the thing." I say nervously "I was sort of - um - in the infirmary."

"Wait what! Why?" He growls and instantly his arms go around me and he pulls me into his lap as he sits on the bed.

"Well you know the smashed windows?" I ask and he gives me a confused nod. "That happened while I was standing next to them."

"What?!" He shouts and tightens his grip on me.

"I was in there getting stuff for Willow but then I hear a knock on the windows. I turn around several rocks smashed all of the windows." I explain with a shrug.

He turns my face towards him with his thumb and gives me a small worried smile, but I can see the anger hiding in his eyes. "Are you okay?"

"I'm okay now. The rock hit my shoulder pretty hard-" Jay pulls down my top over my shoulder, exposing the sickening bruise. He growls before pressing a light kiss on the spot.

"-and the glass cut most of my clothes. They are all healed except where glass got into my ankle. But the doc stitched it up."

"Melody," he whispers starring at my shoulder "you should of told me. I would of taken you to the infirmary, you didn't have to go alone."

"Jay," I laugh softly "you would of flipped if you had seen me covered in blood and cuts. Plus I'm old enough to go the the infirmary alone."

"I know but I'm your mate, I'm here to protect you and taken care of you. Plus I wouldn't of flipped." He smirks at me.

"You would of gone completely insane!" I say slapping his chest playfully, I laugh just imagining his face if he saw me after the windows smashed.

"You're driving me insane that why love." Jay kisses my lips, in an instant my arms are around his neck and his are tightly around my waist.

As he deepens the kiss he moves us so I'm laying down while he hover above me. His lips are warm and soft against mine and the electricity flows between us.

He pulls away sooner than I hoped but he doesn't stop. He sends kisses down my jaw and to my injured shoulder. He places a single soft kiss on the bruise before hovering over me again.

"You're so beautiful. And you beautifully mine!" He whispers and places a single soft kiss to my lips. I can't help but giggle at the complete cheesiness and love.

CHAPTER 20

Jayden and I lay in bed for a couple more hours before he is finally called away to sort out the 'attack'. I know they have to do interviews and searches the grounds. Plus I should prepare for when my family arrives.

I get up when he leaves and change into a pair of leggings and one of Jayden's white shirts. I breathe in his scent and smile.

I can't believe what's happened today. Started off with me telling Jayden I was ready to fully mate to me ending up in the infirmary.

With one final check in the mirror, i walk down the many stairs towards the pack kitchens. I peep my head around the doorway first and gasp internally.

By looking at this room, you would never of realised that it was covered in glass, rocks and blood. It's completely spotless.

I walk in still gobsmacked when a woman comes up to me with a smile. Her hair is pink and up in a tight bun on her head.

"Afternoon Luna, how may I help you?" She says with a bow, Im glad I was use to bowing otherwise it would get very annoying. Although I must I do hate it.

"Oh please call me Melody. I was just looking around, sorry." I almost mumble from my state of shock. This pack does not mess around.

"The cooks and I are about to start dinner for your family Lu-Melody. Willow, Courtney and Lucy are in the upstairs living room." She says, I thank her and leave to find the others.

Courtney is the Delta Female and mates with the Delta Mason. Lucy is the Gamma Female and she is mated to Blaine, the Gamma. I have only met them all once before.

I completely forgot that my family were finally coming down to see me. It's been about 2 weeks since I have seen them. Yes I talk to them almost everyday, but that's not the same.

I find myself upstairs pretty quickly and I hear the girls before I see them. I go to the living room space and see the three girls.

They turn to me and smirk at me.

"Melody hey!" Courtney greets standing up and pulling me over to the couch. I fall back onto the comfy cushioned couch in between Courtney and Willow.

"We were just talking about babies." Willow explains putting her hand on her almost showing belly. I smile at her and nod for them to continue.

I've never really thought about kids much considering I grew up not believing that I had a mate. Now I'm thinking about it; I do want kids. Jayden would be a great father.

I look over to see Lucy holding a young child who looks the spitting image of her, in boy form that is. The kid is fast asleep.

"Right so Melody just to catch you up, Lucy has a 3 year old called Jenny and a 1 year old called Nicky. Courtney hasn't wanted to start a family yet and you already know I'm pregnant." Willow explains pointing around the room as she does.

"Where is Jenny, if you don't mind me asking?" I ask Lucy who smiles and shakes her head quickly.

"Of course not, you are the Luna Queen you know. You can ask us anything and we must answer." She says with a laugh.

"Oh. But please don't think of me as a Luna Queen, you guys are my friends and you're my Beta, Delta and Gamma so we are all together. Call me Melody." I say with a confident nod.

Wow. I'm proud of myself for getting that out there because I've never been one for confrontation or public speaking. Yet I suppose I'll have to get use to that once I'm mated and crowned.

Crumbs!

"Where were we?" Lucy's question pulls me from my thoughts and I quickly listen in.

"I asked what Blaine and Asher were like when you told them you were pregnant." Courtney says looking between the two women.

Willow looks to Lucy and smirks.

"Lets just say, I've never seen Asher so happy then when I told him I was pregnant. He was jumping up and down and kissing my belly. It was weird but sort of cute too." Willow laughs "He can not wait to be a daddy."

"Blaine was almost the same, but for me he is younger than me so I was 19 and he was 17. He found it difficult to come terms with it at first but as soon as he saw Jenny's little face he fell. Then for Nicky he was much more excited!"

"How about you Melody? Have you thought about kids?" Lucy adds and all the girls turn to me.

"Well Jayden and I haven't taken that step yet. We haven't talked about it. But I suppose one day I'll have to have a heir." I say and my heart sinks.

I don't even have a choice whether I have a baby or not. I'm going to have too to keep the bloodline going and the crown passed down. This Queen stuff is way more than I expected.

"I have to go." I say, I can feel my chest tightening and I feel like my lungs are burning. My vision is blurring so as I get up I stumble over something and fall to the floor.

"Melody!" I hear the girls calling me but nothing registers in my brain. My mind is swirling with duties that I have and how my life is going to revolve around the crown.

"Baby." I hear someone whisper in my ear. Sparks fly around my skin as his arms wrap around me, I feel him pick me up but I close my eyes.

"Focus on breathing, in and out okay? Baby please. Just breathe." Jayden voice is calm and soothing. I instantly find myself calming down.

I breathe in and out slowly a few times before I open my eyes. Jayden's face is the first thing in sight and I realise my head lying on his lap.

"I'm okay now, thanks Jay." I say breathing deeply and he grabs my hand.

"What happened Melody?" He asks rubbing his thumb in smoothing circles along my hand. I sit up slowly and move so I sit next to him.

"We were just talking and I panicked about it."

"What were you talking about love, please tell me so I can help." He says kissing my forehead.

"Babies. I panicked because I realise how much of our lives are going to be written out for us. I have no choice on whether I have a baby or not, I will be forced to give you an heir." I say sadly looking down at my hands.

Jayden uses his thumb to lift my chin up to look at him, his blue eyes that are full of electricity are starring straight and me as he speaks.

"Melody, listen to me. Nobody is going to force us to do anything, I've told you before and I'll tell you again; this is us, you and me. Not them. We will have a baby when we are ready to and if you don't want one I will never force you. I am not going to lie to you Melody; it's not going to be easy being King and Queen. We will have duties to perform but nobody will hurt you or force you into anything;

otherwise they'll have to deal with me." He says with a smirk, he flexes his muscles and I literally feel myself melt inside.

I can't believe the girl who grew up believing she was mate-less found the hottest kindest bravest.

"Okay, as long as your by my side Jayden. Also I think I do want kids; as long as their yours." I laugh and Jayden pulls me closer.

"They better be mine Melody." Jayden kisses my lips softly and I smile into the kiss. I wrap my arms around his neck and deepen the kiss but before we get too heated he pulls away.

"Melody, there is something I have to tell you but don't be upset okay." He says and I raise my eyebrow at him "My parents have shut down the borders after the attack on the future Queen" he gestures to me "which means your family won't be able to come down."

"Oh right." I say nodding and looking down at the floor, if I'm honest I hadn't thought about much today. I'll ring them later and speak to them so it's not too bad.

"Hey I have something to show you. Jus follow me and don't say anything." He says and pulls me up, it's only then I realise that we are in his office.

I follow him out the office door and we rush through the maze of corridors of the castle. I wave at all the people we pass and they all bow to us.

I grab Jayden's hand as he starts to speed up and become to fast for me. He looks back and grins at me before whisking me up into his arms.

His pace is faster than mine as we exit the castle and rush through the open grounds then into the trees.

I watch the green trees become a blue as Jayden runs through the forest. I shiver at the cold chill and find myself leaning into Jayden's warm chest.

Jayden comes to a sudden halt and I almost fall out of his arms but, thanks to werewolf reactions, he caught me safely. He slowly puts me on my feet and I look up.

He just smiles and points behind me. I give him a questioning look before spinning around to see nothing except a rope ladder hanging from a tree.

I gasp and look up to see a giant gorgeous tree house above us in the tree line. The tree's branches and leaves are covering most of the house but I can see the beautiful wooden design and a hammock on the balcony.

I turn around and run into Jayden's arms. I hold him tightly and he wraps his arms around me too, accepting my silent thanks.

"Shall we go see it?" He asks placing a kiss on my nose before heading towards the ladder with my hand in his. "Ladies first."

"Why thank you kind sir, anyone would believe you are a prince." I say in a posh tone as I mount the wobbly ladder and start to climb.

"And anyone would believe you are a princess by the beauty you behold." Jayden's comes back at me with a posh British accent.

I laugh and shake my head. My mate is crazy. I finally make it to the top and have to push open a hatch door to get inside.

I pull myself up and into my feet but as soon as I see the treehouse up close I almost fall back. I hear Jayden close the hatch door and pull up the ladder behind me but I'm focused on this little treehouse.

From here I can see inside the glass door, I can see a large double bed with beautiful wooden work all around it. The sheets are a gorgeous forest green.

I can also see a wardrobe in the corner and a door to what must be a bathroom. The outside holds a single balcony that stretches around the entire square house.

On my right is a large hammock that sways gently in the afternoon breeze. To my left is a small table with wooden chairs around it.

"I use to spend most of my days in here," Jayden explains holding the door open "It's amazing. It's somewhere where I can be away from my duties and royalty and the pack. It's somewhere away from the internet so I can just be myself and relax. I thought it would be the perfect place for us to mate. It's the first place I wanted to take my mate whenever I met her, but when you arrived there were so many … complications."

I walk over to him and put my hand on his cheek. He gives me a sweet but sad smile, his face sweeps around the room before landing back on mine.

"Obviously we don't have to mate now but I thought it was the perfect time to show you." He says pulling me inside and shutting the door. "We can stay the night if you want; it's so much fun in here in the mornings. No noise but natural noises."

I watch him sit on the edge of the bed and sigh happily as his eyes wander the gorgeous room. I stand in front of him and just smile.

Jayden always takes so much pride in things he does or has. The grin on his face that he gets when he is proud is one of the best jobs I've ever seen.

I reach out and curl a piece of his hair around my finger and his eyes instantly beam over at me. He reaches his hand out and pulls me closer.

"Jayden," he hums in reply "I love it so much. It's amazing. I'm so sorry for all the...complications but no more of them. I plan to stay forever. I want you Jayden. I want to marry you. I want to have babies with you. I want to be your Queen. I want to rule with you by my side. I love you."

His face morphs into one of complete surprise as I say my true feelings aloud. It only takes a few seconds before he throws me in the bed and lies above me.

"I love you Melody." He says kissing me "I can't wait to start my life with you."

I pull his lips back into mine and the kiss soon gets heated. I put my legs around his waist making us impossibly close and I hear his growl of approval.

His lips press hard against mine and I savour every moment. Our battle of dominance is easy over as he wins before he pulls away but only to place a open mouth kiss on my mark.

A pleasurable moan rips out of me and in that second I decide. I want to mate with him now. Right now I'm not in heat, I'm not being pressured by his family. It's just us. This is how I want it.

"Jayden." I whisper and he pulls away then, with lustful eyes, looks at me.

"Sorry I'll stop." He breathe out heavily, trying to calm himself. I pull his face closer by my hand on the back of his head.

"Don't stop Jay." I whisper and he looks at me with conflicted eyes.

"Don't do it for my sake if anyone else's Melody, we'll do it when you are ready." He says stroking my cheek.

"I am ready Jay. I want to start our life." I say pulling his lips back to mine.

~~~

That night one soul become two loving souls combined. They become stronger in every way. Their love becomes impossibly stronger.

Nothing will get in their way.

———————————————
~~~